# Swimming Middle River

And Other Short Fiction

by

# Leah Holbrook Sackett

# REaDLIPS Press

Editors: Della Rey
Jack Odman
Rebecca Brooke
Noreen Lace

Cover Photo: Oliver

Copyright © 2020 ReadLips Press. Los Angeles, Ca.

All Rights Reserved: No part of this book in whole or in part shall be reproduced without written permission from author and publisher.

This is a work of fiction. Any part reflecting persons or events is coincidental.

ISBN: 978-1-7331813-3-4

*Leah Holbrook Sackett*

"Where you come from is gone, where you thought you were going to never was there, and where you are is no good unless you can get away from it"
— **Flannery O' Connor, <u>Wise Blood</u>**

# TABLE OF CONTENTS

| | |
|---|---|
| The Family Blend | 1 |
| Somebody Else in Kentucky | 20 |
| A Point of Departure | 34 |
| Burnt Prairie | 50 |
| I Heart Burt | 68 |
| Man in Black | 72 |
| Swimming Middle River | 91 |
| The Tooth Of It | 98 |
| Liar | 106 |
| Acknowledgements | 128 |

Leah Holbrook Sackett

# The Family Blend

Albert Marrakesh Schittkowski hated his name, but Schittkowski was the best choice his unwed mother could make forty years ago for the hungry babe at her breast. Doreen gazed at the pulsing temple of her son as he fed and debated over the matter of his surname. Her choices were limited: Schittkowski, the name of her pedophile father or Laban, the name of the man who beat her and kicked her from his bed.

To compensate for the surname, Doreen named him Albert, as in Einstein, so her son would have a good male role model. And she hoped his namesake's genius might transfer to her son. Later, when her Albert enrolled in college, Doreen felt vindicated over this choice. She was sixteen and trapped. She craved escape, so she added a name that was exotic: Marrakesh. It was the best smelling coffee in *Gloria Jean's*. Every morning when she opened the store she brewed a pot in the large brass monstrosity of a machine. The grounds found their way under her finger nails, the oils permeated her fingertips; the aroma, swelling with a promise of more, filled her head. The morning music of percolation, accompanied Doreen's ritual of wrapping a paper bag filled with fresh ground Marrakesh beans over her nose and mouth as if she were hyperventilating. Deep and steady, she breathed the earthy fragrance with undertones of chocolate until released from the waves of morning sickness.

But Doreen was always disappointed when she drank the brew and, again, it tasted like coffee. Coffee perplexed her. It smelled divine; yet it tasted nasty. The smells of the Marrakesh beans were intoxicating, but the taste reminded Doreen of her father's stale Folgers' breath in her mouth. As a child, even brushing her teeth did not remove that taste, and Doreen had to incessantly apply Dr. Pepper lip balm to her lips to eradicate the stale smell. Some days she wanted to shove the entire lip balm into her mouth but, mostly, she licked and nibbled on it during applications.

\*\*\*

*Welcome to Alabama the beautiful*, the sign read. Albert had been driving all day only stopping for coffee and to take a piss at truck stops along route AL 69. He had 48 hours to be back in St. Louis to make his offer on the bar. His stomach turned. It was nerves. He told himself it was a lack of food. Taking the Tuscaloosa exit, Albert watched for signs of a Waffle House or Denny's. He'd thought of driving straight to his grandfather's house, but he wasn't ready. I'll feel better after I eat.

The ends of her hair were matted with maple syrup, and her skin had a greasy stratum that only comes from years of working in kitchens. It penetrated her pores and refused to be rinsed away. She wore the comforting smell of bacon like a sweater.

"Welcome to Waffle House. What can I get ya?"

"Coffee, two sugars. Stack of flapjacks."

Albert saddled-up at the counter. All I have to do is drive over there and pay the groveling dues; then I'll have my money. He needed 80k to buy a failing bar in the newly revitalized and gentrified warehouse district in downtown St. Louis. But Albert had crap for credit. The only bank that was going to give him a loan was the family bank, grandpa.

\*\*\*

Albert wiped down the lonely end of the bar: the end with the pretzels, middle-aged guys, and less noise so you could watch the game. The other end of the bar was populated with a small group of a younger set. They'd been hesitant when ordering there beers like they'd walked into the wrong bar, but it was raining outside, so they stayed. He tried to discreetly eye the two hardly legal blondes in the group. The type he no longer stood a chance with unless they had daddy issues. It was girls like that that kept him from coloring over the ever more present gray at his temples and in his hairline. Albert was an aging bartender in a old man's bar. A bar for sale, which meant he'd probably be replaced.

"It's depressing, isn't it?"

Albert turned his attention back to the middle-aged man with deeply receding dark-blonde hair and coffee-stained teeth. His future.

"What?" Albert said. "I haven't been paying attention to the game." He looked up to see the bobbing head of the Blues Hockey color commentator on the old 27" tube TV.

"Nah, I meant being down here, when we use to belong down there with the living."

In that moment, Albert knew he wanted to buy the bar. He didn't want to be just the bartender for the rest of his life, busting his ass for tips. This was his chance to be the owner, to be somebody. He could update the place and bring customers back. All Albert needed was cash.

\*\*\*

Albert hadn't actually seen his grandfather since he was thirteen. That was the last time his mother dragged him to visit the family. Albert hated going home, as Doreen called it. His mom got emotional, inexplicable tears. Half the time Doreen stayed at her sister's home. As a child, Albert didn't understand why they went at all, but by the age of nine he'd figured out the visits were the only way for Doreen to get money. Every time Doreen was over her head in debit or needed a down payment on a car or house, she and Albert made a trip to Tuscaloosa. On the upside, trips to Tuscaloosa were a dip into the freedom pool for Albert. Doreen was distracted and self-involved at Aunt Kathy's. While his mom and Aunt Kathy looked over photographs of the grandmother Albert never met, he and his cousin Margot were left to their own devices, Margot's devices. And Margot's games were different, fun.

    Albert clearly remembered playing "doctor" with Margot. She got to be the doctor, or she wouldn't play. Margot and Albert would climb up into the attic over the back bedrooms that Aunt Kathy used as her pottery studio. It was warm and shadowy with streaks of dusty sunbeams in the Alabama summers and falls. It was cool and sullen in the winter. Albert refused to play in the winter, until Margot found some old blankets in a cedar chest in the corner of the attic. Here they built a little fort, and disrobed. They would disappear into the attic for long stretches of time. No one needed them. Margot was Albert's first introduction to the female form outside of his mother. He would catch a peek of Doreen's brown, rosy nipples and slackened breasts as her robe shook loose while she ironed piles of laundry in front of the T.V. Albert was both disgusted and curious. But Margot was different. Margot let Albert touch her budding milk-white breasts, her small pink nipples. Even as they slowly swelled, Margot's breasts looked nothing like his mom's, not when Margot was at the age of ten, eleven, or even fourteen.

The first time they had played doctor was when Albert was nine. Margot had dragged him by the elbow down the back hall to a box. Albert wondered what was in the box. He'd hoped it would be match box cars, but he doubted it. Margot liked dolls. Then she stood on the box and pulled a short dingy cord to reveal a folding ladder.

"Wow! What is that?"

"It's the ladder to our attic."

"Cool," he said in a long, low whisper.

"Two to go up!" Margot announced and pointed up before she ascended the ladder into the hovering dark hole. Not to be outdone by Margot, or any girl, Albert ascended the stairs his head poking up into the darkness. He paused on the third to last rung and blinked trying to adjust his eyes. There were boxes heaped up four high lining the walls. There was a Christmas wreath in the nearest corner, an old sewing machine, and a long rod that ran the length of the attic just off to the left hand side if you were facing the backyard. Old clothes, some covered in plastic, hung from the pole.

"Come on," Margot hissed at him. She lowered

herself over the entrance and tugged at the ladder. Once Margot and Albert had managed to close up their entrance, they stood awkward in the dark.

"Isn't there a light?"

"What for? It's not like anyone comes up here. Besides I like it dark." And Margot ducked into the rack of clothing.

"Wait, where are you going? What do you do up here?"

"I don't know, Albert. You sure do ask a lot of dumb questions."

"Sorry." Albert didn't want to make her angry. Margot was the only person to play with in Tuscaloosa, for him anyway. He was sure there must be other kids around, but he didn't know any.

"Let's play doctor," Margot said.

Great a bunch of sick baby dolls, maybe I can go downstairs and get a snack from Aunt Kathy.

"I'll be the doctor. You be sick."

"What do I do? Cough?"

"Sure, then take your shirt off and lie down."

"There aren't any spiders up here are there?"

"No. Want a lifesaver?"

"Yeah."

"Well, then lie down. The lifesavers are the medicine. You can't have a lifesaver until I examine you."

Albert stretched out on the dusty floorboards. It felt warm and cozy behind the rack of clothes in the dim light of a Tuscaloosa May. Margo pressed her fingers gently to his throat. She pressed on his chest. When she got to his stomach he giggled and curled up into a ball.

"Stop that," Margot scolded. Albert stretched himself out again. He'd hoped to still get a lifesaver.

"Can I have a green lifesaver?"

"Patients are supposed to be quiet. Shh. I think you may be very ill. But I'll have to take a look," and she unsnapped his jeans.

Albert sat up, "Hey!"

"Well, if you're too big a baby to play." Margot said turning her back to him.

"No, I just. No." And he flung himself back, bumping his head. As Albert reached back to rub the spot on his head Margot tugged on his pants, freeing Albert of both his Levi's and his briefs. Albert froze in part from sheer embarrassment and in part from fear of what to do. Margot did not seem afraid at all. She pulled a tube of lifesavers from her hip pocket.

"You have a terrible illness. And this is the only way to save you," she said as she clicked off the lifesavers one by one and licked them before applying them to Albert's stomach in a trail to his penis. Albert felt tingly and hot. He began to sweat. He was worried he would do something wrong. He was worried he might have to pee. After Margot had completed the path of lifesavers, she pulled her t-shirt off over her head revealing her budding milk-white breasts.

"Touch them," she said, as if she were telling Albert to touch the new velvet pillows on Aunt Kathy's sofa.

"Go ahead. You touch me and I'll touch you."

\*\*\*

That was how Albert explained, to himself, his kinky fetish for that little girl look, for younger women. Albert was nearly old enough to be the father of the nineteen, twenty year-old girls that he chased, the just legal set. He knew he came off a fool at least half the time, but he didn't care as long as they would put their hair up in pig tails and wear knee socks. Women his own age would spit the word pervert at him, with the venom they felt for their own sagging breasts and fat dimpled thighs. Now, here he was back in Tuscaloosa, on his way to visit grandpa and dreaming of Margot.

Albert drove down the dusky streets, hunting for familiar in the twilight and the trees. He hoped to catch a glimpse of Margot at fourteen again. But he wouldn't, that was impossible. He wouldn't even see Margot in her forties. She had run away from home at sixteen with some guy who got her pregnant. No one had heard from her again. Aunt Kathy and Uncle Butch moved to Nevada a few years later. Only the grandfather and his money were left in Tuscaloosa, and now Albert.

Albert sat at a green light before making an abrupt right down Chicory Lane. He had to see it. He had to see Margot's house one last time. After half a block, there it was. It was smaller than he remembered, and it wasn't painted yellow back then. It'd been white with green shutters. Albert stretched across the bucket seats and empty Styrofoam QT cups to look out, up at the wood rot eaves of the attic.

\*\*\*

"Albert," Margot hissed. She was standing in the hall under the access panel to the attic. Albert had just come from the hall bathroom.

"Call me, Kesh," he said as he swaggered towards her.

Margot smirked and waited for Kesh to pull the cord to the access panel. It was unspoken, now, this game, this jaunt to the attic. The game had not changed much over time, but it had been two years since they last saw one another. Margot was fourteen and Albert was thirteen. Once they had ducked under the clothes rack, Albert saw that Margot had added some blankets and a pillow. She was feathering a little love nest. Albert swallowed hard. Margot was always a few steps ahead of him, but he was determined to take the lead. Margot stripped down to her butterfly panties and bra. For the first time Margot had a real bra, not a training bra. Albert couldn't ignore how Margot's body had changed. His stomach began to feel funny. Albert stripped to his only pair of boxers, snagged from his mom's old boyfriend, out of the laundry. They were big, and he had to roll the waistband to keep them on. He waited for Margot to comment.

"Kiss me," was her only response. She didn't

even seem to notice him. They lay in each other's arms and kissed, hard, wet, and sloppy – like adolescents.

When they pulled apart, Albert said, "Do you remember the lifesavers?"

"I've got something better than lifesavers," Margot said.

She slipped her hands into his boxers and pulled his penis free through the fly. Margot kissed her way down his chest and stomach. This time Albert was too nervous to be tickled; yet he still wanted to curl into a ball. As Margot took him into her mouth, Albert's body went rigid with delight, fear. It wasn't long before he came, and Margot wiped the back of her hand across her mouth. Albert had seen pictures of blow jobs in dirty magazines that he and his friends stole from the collections of fathers and older brothers. But he had no idea that Margot would do that to him. He trembled. Margot wrapped herself around him and said, "Let's cuddle."

When Albert woke, he was sure that they were caught. "Albert! Margot! Where are you kids?" Doreen was calling from downstairs. The smell of chicken and dumplings rose in the air. He shook Margot by the shoulder; then realized she was already awake. They listened to Doreen walk back towards the Kitchen; then dressed and quickly left the attic. Margot tiptoed to the back door, opened it and slammed it. "We're home! Anybody here?" she called out. That was easy. Everything was easy for Margot.

***

Idling in front of 1623 Chicory Lane, Albert didn't know what he had expected to find, exactly. But he unearthed fond memories of which he felt ashamed. He cranked the engine, forgetting it was already running, and put it into gear. Albert didn't say goodbye. How do you say goodbye to a house? This trip was harder than he anticipated. He knew getting money from his grandfather would require ass kissing. Albert was not fond of the idea or the old man. But Albert didn't realize how many ghosts were lurking in Tuscaloosa for him. This was life: transient and unfulfilling. He was the selfish survivor, born to ill-fitting circumstance, where family was best forgotten.

It was only a five minute drive to his grandfather's. The past rose out of the shadows in all its Greek revival glory. A two-story, brick monstrosity with towering white pillars and a sweeping porch that presented the double black, lacquered front doors where Nikolaus Schittkowski was waiting for him.

"Took you long enough, Albert," the old man growled from the shadowed doorjamb. He was bent, but remained bulky and large in his old age.

"Sorry, sir. I was reliving some fond memories. And it's Kesh."

"Come in. Sit down. What's your mother up to?"

"She's living in New Mexico with some hippy-green artist."

"Well, that sounds like Doreen."

Schittkowski took Albert by the chin and turned his face side-to-side in the light of the foyer chandelier. "Well, there's no denying you, anyway. Shit, if you don't look just like me."

Albert did not feel complimented.

"Yep, you're a lucky son of a bitch. You got my good looks and my name, instead of that dickhead that knocked-up your mom," Schittkowski said, and waved Albert to follow with a meaty hand, thick fingered and long yellowed nails.

He was the same. The kitchen was the same, not a single update. The *Coca-Cola* bottle opener still hung on the wall over the trashcan. The daisy curtains, now ragged at the edges, stuck to the kitchen window in the humidity. The black pock-mark from some long forgotten accident was still a blight in the white Formica countertop.

"Sit. Coffee?"

"Ah, yes, sir. That'd be great."

Schittkowski grabbed a thick, white mug from the cupboard and set it down in front of Albert. He picked up the tall carafe of coffee from its warming plate and brought it to the table.

"Would you like a hot dog, Albert?" Schittkowski asked while pouring Albert a cup and giving his own mug a warm-up.

"It's, ah. No. I don't think so."

"Suit yourself." Schittkowski set the carafe on

the table and unscrewed the lid, pulling out a hot dog with his gnarled fingers. Albert looked down into his mug. A greasy film swirled across the top of his coffee.

"Why do you have a hot dog in your coffee pot?"

"It cooks 'em. Don't waste water or time that way."

"Doesn't it make the coffee greasy?"

"Eh, don't be a pansy, boy."

Albert took a dutiful sip. He observed his grandfather. It was true enough that they had the same watery blue eyes, the same square jaw line. His grandfather's stature, his face and hands were beaten-down like a rumpled, busted bus seat. Albert sat a little straighter and made a mental note to inquire somewhere about moisturizer.

"Well, when are you going to get around to it? You came here looking for money didn't you?"

"I, ah, thought we'd visit. I haven't seen you since I was thirteen. I don't know why Mom never came back. I don't know why I never came before." Albert's palms were sweating. He wasn't sure how this was going.

"So, you still want my money?"

"Ahem, may I use your bathroom?"

"You remember where it is?"

"Yes. Thank you."

Albert made his way toward the staircase. The wallpaper, once floral, now looked veined and discolored, threadbare rugs lazed about like sleeping dogs, and the excessively large wooden console, good for hide and seek, crouched by the stair; it was all still there. Everything was the same, just old. Climbing the stairs he was escorted by the aging photographs of his mother and Aunt Kathy as little girls. There were photos of his grandfather when he still had his looks with the grandma he never met. He could tell that his mother favored her mother in looks. The journey to the bathroom was like hitting a familial rewind button. Dressing the stair and the halls were photographic evidence of a happy, unified family he didn't know, his family. They'd gathered, posed with linked arms, and forced smiles, again and again. He could hear his mother's nervous laugh lifting from the walls.

    A light was on in the master bedroom. He'd always been afraid of that room as a kid. Now, standing in the middle of the room, he surveyed it looking for that something scary. The vanity was a heavy piece of oak that weighed down the room. It was littered with remnants of an old man, prescription bottles, a dingy handkerchief, and a tube of Icy/Hot that permeated the room. This was always an old man's room. Albert crossed moonlight and streetlight that filtered through the floor to ceiling shutters; not once could he remember these being open. He fingered the dungy sheets, and took count of the items on the night stand: a brass lamp, a handful of change, an old Westclox double bell alarm clock, a nearly empty water glass, and a framed photo of Margot when she was eleven.

*** 

"Albert, you are underfoot in this kitchen," Aunt Kathy complained.

"Where's Margot?" Doreen asked him.

"I don't know."

"Why don't you go find her and the two of you can walk down to Dewey's and get a gallon of ice cream to go with the peach cobbler I made," Doreen said.

"Yeah, where is Margot? She's always disappearing," Aunt Kathy said to the room at large.

"Now, be quiet. Don't wake your grandfather. I don't need him being cranky when I'm trying to ask him for a loan."

Albert left the kitchen with a five dollar bill tucked into the front pocket of his jeans for vanilla ice cream. He looked out the window, but didn't see Margot. He decided to go check the bathroom. Girls are always in the bathroom, he thought. Before he even reached the bathroom he noticed the door was open and the light was off. Then he heard a low murmur from his grandfather's room. He stepped quietly, careful not to make a sound in his new Puma tennis shoes. He pretended he was a spy like James Bond. He reached the door frame and let his eyes adjust to the dark, then pushed his face further into the room. His grandfather was sitting up on the bed. His grandfather was the one murmuring. Was he talking in his sleep? Sitting in his sleep? Then the light from the shutters caught the blond head of Margot rising from his lap. She looked straight through Albert. His heart was pounding in his chest. He ran down the stairs and out of the house. He wanted to kill his grandfather. He wanted to hurt Margot. Instead he ran till he was out of breath. Then Albert dropped to the pavement on his hands and knees, the sickening-thud of bone on unforgiving concrete. And on an unfamiliar street corner he cried. It was getting dark when he started to navigate his way to Aunt Kathy's house. After a few turns, he got his bearings, but he stopped off to throw rocks at a little black poodle that barked incessantly from its yard. Albert hated to go back to his family, but he had nowhere else to go.

"Albert, there you are," Doreen said half scolding, half relieved. "What are you doing here? You missed dinner, and we didn't have any ice cream with dessert."

Margot crossed the living room in silence and went straight to her room.

"Albert?" Doreen pushed for a response.

"Here's your five dollars." Albert pulled the money from his pocket and threw it on the sofa, before storming off to the guest bedroom.

\*\*\*

Sweat from Albert's palm smeared the glass of the framed photo. He remembered, not that he had really ever forgotten. He'd told himself it wasn't what he thought. He was paranoid, because of the games he and Margot played. It was dark. How could he be sure? But now, in this place, nearly 30 years later, he was sure. He was sure that he'd been betrayed, that his rival was his own grandfather. Albert smashed the frame on the edge of the nightstand. He pulled free the smiling image of Margot in pigtails. His hand shook not to crush it, and he stuffed it inside the pocket of his flaking leather jacket. Albert descended the stairs at a gallop ready to jack his grandfather in the jaw, to claim what was rightfully his.

When Albert reached the kitchen an open checkbook lay on the table next to his cup of coffee. Albert stalled.

"Trust you found the bathroom alright?"

He was packed with anger and anxiety. Albert thought he might puke, instead he picked up the coffee cup and drained it.

"That greasy flavor is growing on you. I knew I liked you, boy."

Schittkowski pulled a hot dog out of the pot, and took a big bite. He started to chuckle. His grin turned into a grimace, and the chuckle was cut short. Albert felt the world slow down, as he watched Schittkowski slam a hand on the table. The coffee cups jumped, and the spoons jangled. The old man rose, staggering from his chair. His eyes were wide and his hand went to his throat. The words "choking" and "Heimlich maneuver" crossed Albert's mind. Instinct kicked-in with a renewed surge of adrenaline. Albert embraced his grandfather from behind and began what he thought must be the right movement, a violent thrust against the diaphragm with his fists. Schittkowski was heavy. He slipped in Albert's arms with each inward thrust. They tumbled to the floor. Albert tightened his grip.

"Come on, you son of a bitch. Come on," Albert shouted as he struggled on the floor with his grandfather convulsing in his arms. Albert pulled himself free and stumbled back and up against the counter. He was raging and crying. He paced the floor.

"Shit! Shit," and kicked Schittkowski in the gut. A large piece of hot dog was jettisoned across the floor. Schittkowski lay on the floor wheezing. Albert kicked him again and again. The old man drooled and moaned and laughed.

# Somebody Else In Kentucky

      I was somebody else in Kentucky. Well, at least I tried to be. But traveling is always messy. I hate sleeping on a hotel bed; it's like sleeping on an oversized Ritz Crackers box, covered with a paper towel. Yet, when you sign in at the front desk of a hotel you can be anyone, anyone at all, whoever you dream up. So, when my best friend Jackie asked me to tag along to Kentucky, I said yes.

      Jackie is a mechanic at a Chevy dealership here in St. Louis. A job opportunity for Senior Mechanic opened up in Kentucky, so we picked up and headed east for Lllville. "Lllville." That's how they say Louisville down there. You want to smack people on the back of the head and help them spit the word out.

It took me two and half hours to pack while I listened to the Weather Channel. These things require planning, you know. In the end, I packed a rainy, cold, and warm weather option for each day of the trip. Oh, and a lot of shoes. It is better to be safe than sorry, as they say. And I believe it. I calculate everything. I was raised on forewarnings and formulas. Such as the formula for success: go to college, get a job, and get married. I followed it perfectly. But the "get-married" thing just didn't happen. Granted, I'd only been out of college for two years, but my relationships had been as romantic as a wait in line at the Department of Motor Vehicles, yet rarely lasting as long. I began to wonder if it was me. Did I set up impossible expectations for love? I admit I spent most of my evenings with my nose in a book, which probably lent to lofty ideals of love and little opportunity to meet Mr. Right. Then one day, when I was sitting in my little gray cubicle in a big gray building, typing away in the grid of my Excel file, I received yet another office-wide invite to happy hour. This time it came from the newest bride of the twenty-third floor of Property/Casualty, Stacy.

"Come on. It will be fun. You have to celebrate my engagement."

*Oh, I do, do I?* "Of, course."

I knew the fun girls of the floor frequented the nearby bars and clubs. I would listen to their chatter choked with giggles during lunch as they confessed the lurid details of their illicit affairs. I sat at the end of the table chewing my turkey sandwich and devouring articles in Cosmo about the great sex I wasn't having. *Hmmm, One-third of people report that they have better and more frequent sex on vacation, according to the 2004* National Leisure Travel Monitor.

I decided the happy hour would be an entertaining anthropological study of these *fun* girls and their slutty behavior. I also decided to check my make-up. That afternoon, I think I wore a path in the gray, commercial-grade carpet between my cubicle and the ladies room. Under the pulsating fluorescent light, I reapplied and reapplied my make-up. I fidgeted with my gray wool suit. I brushed out my hair, clipped it back in my barrette, and then I brushed out my hair again. Any way I arranged me I still looked less than glamorous. I returned to my desk and calculated risk of a flood plain actually flooding in the next 10 years. That's what I do for a living. I am an actuary for an insurance company. I calculate the odds that some set of circumstance may or may not happen. Like, whether I will have a date for New Year's Eve.

Happy hour turned out just like lunch hour with the addition of dried out chicken drummies drowning in hot sauce. The fun girls of the twenty-third floor were perched at the bar flirting with the bartender. I wilted at a wooden table with wax build-up, a Cherry Coke and a small plate of the crappy drummies. I missed my *Cosmo* and debated how long I would have to sit there before I could make an excuse to leave. Then I wondered if they would even notice.

That's when Jackie approached me. Looking to be in his mid 30s, he had hair like hay at harvest time. Dimples punctuated his toothpaste-commercial smile like exclamation points in one of my Spanish romance novels. He rested his strong ruddy hands, with immaculately groomed fingernails, on the back of the wooden chair opposite me and inquired if I was using it. I gaped and waved for him to remove the chair. And do you know what he did? He sat down. He sat down and he talked. I stayed in that bar later than anyone else from the office. They didn't notice, but I didn't care.

The most amazing thing was Jackie just kept talking. We talked every day. Soon he became my best friend—just friends—and I'm not really sure why. Whenever he was in-between relationships, his interest in me swelled. Believe me, I noticed. Hell, I tingled when his eyes sketched nimbly across my body, and I swooned over his smooth voice when he called me "Katie" instead of Kate. Was it me? Had I sent the wrong message?

But I also wondered if Jackie was a gentleman or a coward. He was not a gambler. He'd lived in the same house all his life. He bought his parents' house when they retired and moved to Lake of the Ozarks, so his dad could fish while his mother spent her days shopping at the outlet malls. He didn't even change the décor. He never changed a thing except girlfriends. He had never even been outside of St. Louis until I directed him to Kentucky.

"Indiana?" Jackie blurted as we crossed the state lines.

"Indiana, we named the dog Indiana," he grimaced in his best Sean Connery. I giggled in amusement. It was a game we played. He quoted movies. I named them. He'd seen more movies than Ebert and Roper. Jackie lived through TV and film.

We were rolling east down Interstate 64, orange Kodak flashes of lightning snapped in the night sky to the south of us.

"Glad I packed that jacket."

I started calculating our chances of being in a tornado. There had been 59 killer tornadoes, resulting in 405 fatalities in Kentucky. The deadliest was on March 27, 1890, when 76 people were killed in and around Louisville. Those figures didn't seem too bad, but I kept my eye out for ditches on the side of the road.

Jackie drove the first stretch. I drove the second stretch, exhausted. I'd been up all night finishing reports for work. Sitting behind the wheel, I debated just how good an idea cruise control was; it just makes it too easy to fall asleep. Plus, I had taken Dramamine. More than two hours in a car and I'm off-road retching. In addition to my increasing sleepiness, streaks across the windshield created a glare in my line of vision.

"God, I'm tired. I keep hallucinating. I keep thinking I see bridges and overpasses," I yawned with watery eyes.

"You, too?" Jackie asked amused. "I thought it was just me. Scary how we can talk about seeing things that aren't there and not be afraid of each other's driving."

"Yeah, did you see the train? I thought I saw a locomotive coming down the left lane straight at us. I knew it wasn't there, but I thought I saw it anyway," I babbled. "Aaah, no. I only saw bridges," Jackie laughed.

We rolled through the night. Jackie rolled down his window a crack, reclined, took casual drags off his Camels and ashed out the window. The thin whistle of the wind through the window warned me to stay awake; Its cool brush upon my arms reinforced the stiffness in my back. We rolled on, listening to a Guns N' Roses CD, *Appetite for Destruction*; Jackie's favorite.

He is all about nostalgia. The way he holds on to the past is part of his charm. The wheels raced with every whine of Slash's guitar, with every sing along, and with every beat of my heart. We rolled away from St. Louis, my head humming, slipping. I wondered who I would be in Kentucky, and when I returned to St. Louis if I could return as that somebody else.

The night became a blur once we arrived, first nights in a different state always do. I think it's part of the magic of checking into a strange hotel in the wee hours of the morning. The sky was still wrapped in a blanket of deep blue in the west, but the chirp and whistle of birds broke with the light from the east. My internal clock was grinding at a sluggish pace as we signed in at the front desk. I suggested it would be fun to sign in under assumed names. He grumbled writing, *Jackie Corwin and Katie Moore.*

When we got to our room, he claimed the double bed by the desk. I got the double closest to the bathroom. Plenty of nights, Jackie, drunk, had slept on my couch, but this was our first time in a hotel. I thought it might be different, feel different. It didn't. I slept most of the day, waking only long enough to eat breakfast in bed.

"I got orange juice, coffee—I don't know how you like it—and donuts," Jackie announced striding across the room. He loomed above me, a blur in my sleepy blindness. I blinked and rubbed the sleep in my eyes as he unloaded a tray wafting with breakfast aromas. Sleepy speech nearly slipped my tongue. I could marry this man, I thought. Thankfully, I'm practiced at editing the pulse of my heart. I sat up in bed, all Morphean mumbles.

"I've never eaten breakfast in bed before," I smiled. Happily, I broke off a sticky piece of chocolate donut. I don't actually like donuts or drink coffee, but I guess he didn't know that.

"What?" he said with a frown as he added sugar to his coffee.

There I was with breakfast in bed; I never would have thought this moment was possible. I never was a breakfast person. It made me queasy. I found myself erecting ivory towers; hoping Jackie would bestow upon me long awaited affections. We conversed casually the rest of the morning. He set off to his interview. I stayed in bed and watched the Weather Channel before dozing off.

Heavy and sweaty from too much sleep, I awoke mid-afternoon and peeled back the scratchy floral print coverlet. I showered, dressed, and began to write in my journal. I recorded the morning breakfast with the eagerness of a schoolgirl in love. The lock clicked, and I smiled at the shiny, scratched brass knob. He was back, animated and full of news. Jackie slung two newspapers on my bed and talked about his interview, the possibilities of the job, the apartment listings in the paper, and the people he met.

"The receptionist was really cute. She invited me out this evening. I told her you'd have to come along.

"My heart, still in mid-leap from his return, crashed upon the cheap carpet under my feet. I hoped my face hadn't fallen with the same force of gravity. The plans were made and there was no turning back. I had to meet this competition, as I saw it, and competition was not how I wanted to see it. Angry with myself, I was confounded about how to deal with my emotions. I wanted things to be different from St. Louis. I wanted to be different. But how?

Jackie napped as I quietly cried into my journal.

My eyes watched his slumbering face. I wondered what his dreams were as my dreams faltered. He rolled away from the caress of my eyes. In time, he grew restless, awoke, and took an interest in my lengthy journal entry. Torn away from self-pity, I felt my heart thawing. I felt him watching me. I wondered how I had gotten this far into falling for him, and I wondered if I was in an abusive relationship with myself.

Getting ready for dinner, I looked into my make-up bag and surveyed the mascara, eye shadow, lipstick, powder, and blush, wishing there was a magic wand in my arsenal as well. Taking one final look at myself in the mirror, I went to my suitcase to pick out something that would translate as "hot." A black v-neck cashmere sweater was all I had that translated to anything remotely "hot." But whom was I dressing up for? I wasn't dressing up for Jackie. I was dressing up for that girl I was to meet. It was only natural for me to feel jealous about a possible future co-worker of his. Someone that would have him every day, all to herself, while I would be alone in St. Louis.

We arrived at the pool hall first. Like a hunter, I recognized her the moment she walked in, this girl I had never met. I recognized her before Jackie did. She wore a black Alice Cooper concert t-shirt, a pair of acid-wash jeans, and black boots. Her bleached hair was pulled back in a ponytail that accentuated her roots. She looked cheap, just like all of Jackie's girls. She walked straight up to Jackie and slugged him in the arm while giving me a sidelong glance.

"Let's shoot some pool. I'll get the table. You get a bucket of beers," she said to Jackie.

"Okay," he said and hoisted himself off his stool.

The night played out with Pat Benatar and Garth Brooks dominating the jukebox. Jackie lost interest in our female companion every time she leaned over to take a shot and revealed her love handles. I was relieved. I calculated every shot, and let Jackie win. And I didn't have love handles. Jackie became focused on giving me pointers on all my shots. On the way back to the hotel, we stopped off at a Kroger. Jackie wanted a six-pack. The digital clock on the dash read 12:00 midnight: time was running out. We were heading back to St. Louis in the morning. I had to move this relationship into a romance. I had to do something and I had to do it now.

"Let me go in and get it," I chirped, unbuckling my seatbelt.

"Okay," he said handing me a crumpled twenty from the front pocket of his tight-fitting jeans.

Once inside, I walked the entire grocery store looking for what I wanted. I walked up and down aisles, past cornflakes and baby formula. I didn't know where I was or how far was I willing to go. I paced past frozen pizza, ice cream, bagels, milk, and chips, searching. In front of a refrigerator case, I stared at cans of Busch Beer, chewed my lip, and rubbed my arms to keep warm.

I made a choice. I was a girl. No. I was a woman. I was someone I wouldn't have to be tomorrow if I didn't want to be.

I opened the cooler and grabbed a six-pack, turned on my heel, and tramped off to the pharmacy. Annoyed to find the condoms were kept under lock and key in a glass case, I lingered, making my decision about brand, style, and quantity. I went in search of a Kroger employee. I found one, but it took a total of three people to discuss, locate the key, then escort me to the case for my selection. I would have felt awkward at home, but here I felt my purchasing power and my anonymity from them and myself. I had never walked so straight, so tall in all my life. My head high, I was a beautiful, independent woman, a stranger. I carried my six-pack of beer and blue pack of Trojan lubricated condoms to the cashier. I paid with cash and a smile. I handed the crumpled twenty, damp with the sweat of my hand, to the teenage checkout girl. She had one of those silver baby-feet pins on the breast of her uniform and a blush on her face. Walking out, I heard the giggling over my purchase and I felt empowered.

I got into the car and put the bag by my feet. The drive back to the hotel was silent. No music. No talking. I guess Jackie was tired. Whereas I was busy getting acquainted with this woman in the car, this woman with the condoms. Back at the hotel room, Jackie tossed his keys onto the desk. He paused when he grabbed a beer out of the bag, then flopped down on the bed, grabbing the remote and flicking on the TV. He stopped on a *Dukes of Hazard* rerun. I cracked open a beer for myself, still standing. I choked down a sip. Eventually, I hung up my jacket, kicked off my black leather loafers, and took another slug of beer. I bounced onto the bed next to Jackie. He was propped up on pillows and he turned to watch me in amusement. I handed him my beer and began jumping up and down on the bed. I laughed at myself. I felt like I was playing the part of a white-trash girl in somebody else's life. I took out my barrette. My hair fell loose and playful in my face with every bounce.

"It's getting hot."

"Why don't you take your clothes off if you're hot?" Jackie questioned devilishly.

*Why don't I?* Throughout the episode of the *Dukes of Hazard,* I shed clothing. The General Lee spun its tires; I whipped off a black alligator belt and yanked off my charcoal gray socks. My toenails were painted Rocket Fire Red and lit up against my fair skin and the thin, graying sheets. A few bounces later and I was taking a trip to the bathroom. Jackie and I were barreling through the six-pack. Daisy Duke was gagged and bound to a chair; I was stripping off my jeans and slipping under the covers. After another beer, and Daisy's release, I was hopping on the bed in my sweater and pink satin panties. Jackie continued to lie propped up on the flat pillows beneath me. He flashed his teeth, bared his smile.

The Dukes saved the day, and I slinked out of my bra without removing my sweater. The pink bra with a little red rose sailed across the room and landed with the rest of my wasted clothing. I wanted to do something, but what? I wanted to be a sexpot, but the moves were awkward and clumsy. Jackie clicked the TV off.

"Turn out the light," he said, suddenly quite serious. He had not moved an inch, and lay in bed fully clothed. Lying next to me in the dark, Jackie began to strip. Then taking my hand, he pressed it into the growing rise in his boxers. slowly I rubbed and fondled. Groping through the darkness like a drowning voyager grappling for a lifesaver, I reached out.

The rough skin of his hands slipped under my sweater, caressing my breasts with a firm and gentle pressure. The weight of him pressed into me, and with wet gulps his mouth swallowed me bit by bit. Grinding in a long forgotten rhythm, I let go. Jackie collapsed on top of me, sweaty.

"I need to smoke," he said.

A cotton-mouthed *I love you* weighed upon my tongue. My lips brushed against his ear. Jackie reached out to the bedside table and lit-up.

He exhaled, "I didn't know we could be those kinds of friends, Katie."

Another drag burned a hole in the night. I felt about for my panties with my feet, kicking the twisted sheets to the bottom of the bed, and wrangled them back on. I rolled away; ran my hands through my hair. Jackie stubbed out his cigarette. I had tried to be somebody else, but he was still Jackie. And there we were, the three of us in bed, and all of us in our underwear.

"I had you figured all wrong," he mused.

I could not nor did I care to hear any more of what Jackie would say at long intervals. That night, we slept a dance that moved us closer together out of a need for body heat and a desire to avoid the wet spot, but we never touched.

# A Point of Departure

Uncle Ned would be waking up soon, and he would be angry to find Kitty using the most popular color to paint one of the dented coffins.

She needed to finish. She needed a cigarette. Kitty stepped out into the thick August dawn. The wooden-framed screen door slowly, quietly swung close behind her. She was a little light-headed from the ***Pretty in Pink*** paint fumes. Looking down at her small, paint speckled hands, Kitty picked at the paint gunk in her cuticle beds and under her nails. Then she stretched up her arms, reaching to the sunlight that warmed her face and exploded in red blotches on her closed eyelids. Kitty listened to the birds' chirp in the woods behind their lot. Opening her eyes, she turned and squinted into the dark timbered, slanted workshop that hung off the back of the white, wooden-framed house. Kitty was figuring how long it would take for the paint to dry.

The worst of the dented coffins, made by the Chattanooga High shop students working as interns at Uncle Ned's ***Sweet Dreams Pet Cemetery***, were Kitty's property. The guys in her class that signed up for this internship were interested in three things: getting to horse around with the dead cats and dogs, getting high off the paint fumes, and gawking at Kitty's breasts, which continued to swell each year. She was definitely shaping up to be her Momma's daughter. With such distractions in place, the number of poorly constructed coffins was generally two or three a month. Kitty was actually impressed at how Uncle Ned was able to motivate and instill fear in these degenerate young men to get twenty plus suitable coffins a month.

It was more than anyone else had ever gotten out of them.

The quality coffins were sold to other pet cemeteries all throughout the Bible belt, and Uncle Ned made a fair profit. He said only eccentric old folks and parents of spoiled brats would spring for a plot in a pet cemetery. He couldn't make a living off the burials alone.

But it's surprising how many eccentrics and brats there were even in a small town outside of Chattanooga. Uncle Ned had been a quiet fixture in the background of Kitty's life until her mother walked out on them when Kitty was eight-years-old. Uncle Ned felt it his duty to parent her, which was primarily accomplished through his rambling thoughts on death and money while he was sawing, sanding, or painting a small coffin. As a hard-working Southern Baptist, Uncle Ned believed that idle hands mischief makes. So, as soon as Kitty's mother was out of the picture, he had Kitty in the shop painting coffins. Kitty didn't mind. Kitty liked playing with the pastel paints, and the smell of the Georgia pine. It was better than sitting alone all day in the house or out in the yard waiting for her Momma to return from Atlanta.

Kitty never was creeped-out by the coffins since she had been raised right up with them.

She used to use some of the dented ones as cradles for her dolls before she'd been put to work out in the shop.

That was when her Momma was still at home. Kitty only remembered details about her mom. Little things, like the way she smelled of Big Red gum and had shiny, sticky, glossed lips when she tucked Kitty in bed at night. She could still feel the tickle of her Momma's bleached, blonde splint ends falling like a veil over her face. Momma would kiss her just at the hairline and whisper right into that kiss, "Good night, sweet Kitty," before going down to the Chattanooga Choo Choo tavern.

Kitty also remembered climbing in bed with Momma at Noon on the days that followed, and the smell of smoke mated with a stale whiff of vomit. Kitty would quietly enter the darkroom shrouded from sunlight with heavy rose-colored Chenille curtains. Her bare feet nimbly padding across the floor as she carried in Momma's breakfast tray holding a tall glass of milk, dry toast with honey on it, and a shot glass of Pepto Bismo. Kitty called this a Momma breakfast. Momma called it salvation and Kitty, her angel, pressing a hard kiss into Kitty's hairline with dry, cracked lips and rough breath. These were the kinds of memories Kitty had of her mother Pearl, not long involved memories like the kind that start with "I remember the time my Momma took me to …" or "Once, just my Momma and me…" Her memories were fragmented but vivid. Kitty wondered when Momma would find her Daddy.

Kitty wanted to go and wait with Momma for her Daddy to walk in the door of that tavern because it seemed to Kitty that was where her mother kept expecting him to turn-up.

Kitty took the last drag off of her Camel then field stripped it, and walked back into the dimly lit workshop. She was working under the light of a bare bulb from her Hello Kitty lamp. The pink shade lay at her feet as she perched upon the stool to finish painting the name on the coffin. Kitty enjoyed painting the little coffins and detailing them with designs of flowers and vines. She loved inhaling the fragrance of sawed and hewn Georgia pine, and Uncle Ned stopped harping Kitty about wasted time and paint when he realized little old ladies would pay more for a coffin with detailed curlicues, hearts, and flowers. But this morning, she didn't dare turn on the overhead halogen lights for fear the hum or light might wake Uncle Ned.

This coffin was not for a customer. Kitty had a hobby or a damn bad habit as Uncle Ned would call it, of finding and burying roadkill. Kitty couldn't bear to see a raccoon, opossum, cat, or dog dead on the side of the road with no final home. She would drive around with her boyfriend Caleb on Saturday mornings in her old, Chevy Nova looking for victims of Friday night's drinking and driving. Caleb would wait in the car behind the driver's wheel and smoke while Kitty would shovel and scrape up the animal into a black Hefty trash bag. Typically, they didn't find too many animals intact enough for Kitty to give a proper burial, which suited Caleb just fine. He didn't get Kitty's obsession with everything having a final home; to him, it was just creepy. But what he did get was time out on lonely, dusty roads with Kitty's large breasts.

So, Kitty scouted and scooped while Caleb waited for his intervals of groping as they drove down dusty roads.

Kitty was always more agreeable to his fondling after they found a right road kill fit for burial. In Kitty's mind, Caleb was another cocky jock but, worse, he knew he was getting out of there on a football scholarship and never coming back. This provided him with the excuse to use people he would never have to answer to, including Kitty. But Kitty couldn't pull herself away from watching Caleb's calculated dramas unfold, each time impressed that she had not seen his latest offense coming. Caleb always got what he wanted. Kitty always got nervous and another pack of cigarettes.

Kitty finished painting POOCHIE on the coffin. Poochie was the name she decided to give this little flattened Lhasa. Kitty named all the animals she buried. Turning off her lamp, she left the small coffin to dry as she showered. She heard Uncle Ned stirring in the kitchen. She wanted to get out of there before he could hassle her about her Saturday morning ritual. Uncle Ned had a way of making Kitty feel guilty about everything. She tried to skulk past the kitchen doorway and down the hall to the bathroom, but Uncle Ned was waiting for her.

"Kitty," he said.

"Yeah, Uncle Ned."

"What are you doing?" He put down the spoon he had been using to stir Coffeemate into his mug of coffee from a 3-day old pot, watching him drink that crap made Kitty choke.

"I'm just going to take a shower and go out, as usual, Uncle Ned," she dropped her gaze to the cracked, yellow linoleum floor that filled the growing expanse between them.

"With Caleb, again."

"Yes." Kitty rolled her eyes.

"I don't know, Kitty. I'm beginning to wonder why a boy like Caleb would want to spend his Saturday mornings digging up and burying roadkill with you."

"He's nice." Now, even as she said it, she knew Uncle Ned knew better, everyone in town knew better. Kitty was not in the mood to go down this road again, and quickly exited the doorjamb to the kitchen and went to take her shower.

Every few weeks, Uncle Ned was careful to remind Kitty of the evil that sex would bring, such as illegitimate children like herself. His accusations of promiscuity began three years ago when Kitty turned thirteen. That was when Uncle Ned had decided that along with the bra he was forced to take her downtown to buy at Kmart, it was also time for the talk.

However, his talk had little to do with men and women and was more about her Momma. "Your Momma and Daddy weren't never married, you see," he turned in his seat to face her while pulling a Twenty from his worn-leather wallet with Jesus' face branded into it. She stared up into his grimy, dusty brow. A thin Georgia pine curl hung in his hair. ***What is he talking about?*** He rubbed his hand down his face and turned to look out the windshield.

"Your mother didn't take any mind as to who she went with. And she didn't take much care in her soul neither. Now that's the worse I'll ever say bout her, cause she's my sister. And though she is a sorrow to me and the good Lord, I love her. But don't you go and get ideas to be cattin around all over town, 'cause you got this here bra now. You understand? Now go and get it. And be quick."

Kitty just focused in tighter on the Georgia Pine curl brushing against his forehead pricked with sweat and wondered how had her swelling young breasts become more than an embarrassment, but now some sort of accomplice in the blight upon her Momma's soul.

"Go on." He thrust the bill at her.

She took it and jumped out of the old, beat-up pick-up truck and walked into the store. Uncle Ned's speech had the desired effect. It left Kitty none the wiser to the birds and the bees, ashamed of her maturing body and now fearful of and for her Momma. Kitty had wanted to get a pretty pink bra with a flower on it like the other girls at school. But now that she stood before the sea of billowing bras, mostly white with a few pink ones, followed by a small congregation of black lacy ones tucked in the corner like a seductive shadow over the entrance to the dressing rooms, Kitty felt there wasn't any room for pink in her life. And she was awash with the memory of the morning after her Momma had left.

Kitty had slept in that hot summer morning. She always slept in, because Momma slept in. It was shortly before Noon when Kitty walked down the hall to the kitchen to make Momma's breakfast tray. She entered the kitchen to find Uncle Ned emptying the liquor bottles into the sink and throwing out Momma's shot glass collection. The white kitchen sheers with the pink pansies embroidered on them waved weakly over the kitchen window with each stilted breeze. Kitty was confused and annoyed at Uncle Ned being found anywhere besides the workshop.

"Hey, those are Momma's. I need one of those for her, Pepto," Kitty said.

"No, you don't."

"Momma's going to want it."

"Your Momma don't want nothin' in this house. Now, go fetch her damned bras and nylons off the towel rack in the bathroom and throw them in this here trash can," Uncle Ned said.

Kitty gaped at him. Uncle Ned had lost his mind. She turned and ran down the hall to rouse Momma to put a stop to Uncle Ned's antics. *Why did he have to come out of the workshop? Why didn't her Daddy show-up and take them away from Uncle Ned's?* Kitty burst into her Momma's room, her complaints in progress.

"Momma, get up, Uncle Ned is throwing…" she started.

Kitty stopped mid-sentence looking at Momma's room. The dresser drawers were pulled out and emptied. The bed stripped bare. *Where's Momma?*

"Momma, Momma," Kitty hollered, running past the dark empty bathroom back down the hall to the kitchen.

"Where's my Momma?"

"Atlanta," he emptied the last bottle of vodka. "Atlanta at last. She said she was going to look for your Daddy. She got it in her head that he's still in Atlanta, driving that soda truck. Don't expect her back, Kitty." He dropped the empty bottle into the trash can full of Momma's clothes.

"Please, do as you're told, Kitty.

We don't need none of this stuff anymore," he said.

Kitty walked in a daze to the bathroom. She took her Momma's bra down from the rack, but she didn't return to the kitchen.

She went back to her room. That was the last time Uncle Ned and Kitty spoke of Momma, except for the vague allusion Uncle Ned made to Kitty's Momma every evening at the supper table during Grace.

Standing under the A/C vents in the glinting light of Kmart, Kitty began to see her Momma through Uncle Ned's eyes. Momma was not a heartbroken woman who went in search of Kitty's Daddy. She was an immoral woman who went looking for sex. Kitty couldn't get this image of her Momma into her head. She couldn't love this image. Kitty did the only thing she could think of to protect herself and Momma. She bought a nice, plain white bra that day as a defense of her Momma's virtue. She would prove her Momma was a good woman.

But now, at sixteen-years-old standing in front

of the full-length mirror hung on the back of the bathroom door, she questioned herself. She stared at her naked body. She wondered if she was a good woman. She ran her hands over her breasts, squeezing, holding, and thinking about Uncle Ned, Caleb, and Momma. When she looked at her breasts, she felt Uncle Ned's shame and Caleb's desire.

But most of all, Kitty felt a longing for her Momma. These were her Momma's breasts. She knew well enough her overgrown double Ds were one of the few things Momma had given to her. Kitty also bleached her hair blonde like Momma, but she wore it in a pixie cut.

Long hair was too much trouble in the workshop; it always got in the paint. Kitty released her grip and her mind and stepped into the shower.

Kitty was able to escape further conversation with Uncle Ned by moving quickly and quietly.

The day was growing sultry and dripping in August heat. She unlocked the trunk of the car and was hit with the smell of years of nicotine mixed with hot rubber and decaying dog. She carefully lifted the little coffin into the trunk of her Nova next to the stiff Poochie wrapped in the trash bag. She had to nudge the dead dog closer to the old spare tire to get the coffin in the trunk.

Kitty pulled into Caleb's long gravel driveway and slid over to the passenger's side. Caleb tossed a shovel into the back seat and then got in to drive. It was

Caleb's job to dig the graves. He didn't mind, though, because those were the days that Kitty was willing to go all the way. He'd made sure to buy a pack of Trojans on Thursday at the BP right after he and Kitty had found the dead dog outside the Chattanooga Choo Choo tavern.

They drove out past Mr. Woods' farm. Unloaded the dog, coffin and shovel, and headed into a small grove of trees. There was a hill on the other side of this grove. Kitty liked to use this spot to bury her roadkill pets. Uncle Ned would not allow Kitty to bury these animals in his Pet Cemetery. He claimed it was only for paying Christian customers. Kitty had no idea who might have owned this hill she had sanctioned as her own. But it was pretty much out of the way, and she never put up any headstones, which is why she painted the names on the coffins.

Kitty watched Caleb as he stood shirtless under the Sun, digging the grave. She liked to watch the ripple of the muscles in his back with each dig. Caleb dug a shallow grave, and they settled Poochie into the ground. Kitty slid her slender fingers up and down the lid, satisfied with her paint job. She outlined the fine script of Poochie. It was pretty, she thought, even death looks better in pink. She didn't have anything to say about Poochie. So, she brushed the loose dirt from her knees then began to unpack the bologna and mayonnaise sandwiches and Pabst Blue Ribbon beer from her backpack. Caleb covered the coffin with the fresh dug earth. When the coffin was sufficiently covered, Caleb dropped the shovel and stretched out beside Kitty in the grass. He was ready.

He took a swig of warm beer and then grabbed her wrist, taking a bite of her sandwich. With a dramatic toss backward, Kitty swallowed the last slug of warm beer.

The sun warmed her face. She closed her eyes. She was overpowered with the smell of the fresh dug earth and the ever lingering scent of Georgia pine from the coffin. The fragrance of Georgia Pine seemed to fill Kitty's nostrils no matter where she went, expanding in her lungs. Now, it mingled with the sweat of Caleb's body and the smell of warm beer on his breath as he closed over her mouth. His mouth made a hot path down her neck as he unbuttoned her shirt. She reached back unhooking her bra, and he began sucking her nipples. They rolled back into the tall grass. Kitty loved the prickle of the grass on the bare skin of her back. She spread her arms out, liberated by the radiance of the Sun on her exposed pink flesh.

She did not hear the footsteps fast approaching from the tiny grove of trees. Her eyes flashed open as she was snatched by the wrist and yanked up to her feet. Kitty tried to pull her hand free to cover her exposed breasts, brilliantly white under the summer Sun.

"Whore. Whore," Uncle Ned shouted.

Kitty said nothing. She tried to wrangle free. Caleb was already scrambling backward away from them.

Uncle Ned did not address Caleb, leaving Caleb free to run down the hill and across the field to the back of Mr. Wood's property. *Where the hell is he going? Why is he leaving me here?*

Uncle Ned's grip tightened on Kitty's wrist. He glared into her eyes. He said nothing. His large, lanky frame seethed over her. He held her fast with his arm outstretched. They were posed like one of those prize fish photos where men plastered with pride display the whopper they caught. Kitty's hands were dripping with sweat, "You're hurting me," she said. The sweat ran from her fingertips, down her palm, and into his hand. She looked away from his face and down at her shirt and bra lying in the dirt. He pulled her forward to the little grove of trees.

"My clothes," she protested.

He drug her on. She stumbled over roots and rocks. He moved forcefully, quickly through the trees.

She could see his truck parked next to her car as they grew closer to the dirt road. He shoved her towards the car. Kitty fell against it, searing her stomach and chest against the hot metal and glass that had been baking in the sun.

"Drive home," his jaw twitched as he gritted his teeth.

Kitty wanted to protest about her clothes. Standing there half-naked in front of him, she wilted in the heat of his hatred. She was too afraid to do anything other than what she was told.

She couldn't get the car door opened fast enough, get the car started fast enough, or drive fast enough. She cried hard, wrenching sobs as she drove home.

Uncle Ned pulled in right beside her.

Kitty ran into the house and locked herself in her bedroom. She could hear Uncle Ned slam the front door, and then bang around in the workshop.

Kitty cried herself to sleep.

When she woke, Kitty's eyes felt hot and swollen from crying. She had a headache and needed a smoke. Kitty reached over her alarm clock, glaring a tiny, red 11:14 p.m. and felt for a soft pack of Marlboro Lights. "Shit." They were empty. Tobacco flakes fell onto the pilled, thin sheets. Kitty climbed out of bed and grabbed her old Mountain Dew t-shirt off of the floor. The logo was faded and flaked, but it was her favorite. Kitty walked softly to her bedroom door avoiding the creaky spot by the T.V., lay down on the floor and tried to look through the crack at the bottom. She was met with darkness. ***Where is Uncle Ned?*** She couldn't make out any sounds on the other side of the door. Under the hum of the window unit and katydids, Kitty carefully climbed out her bedroom window to get a pack from the car. The car door croaked when she opened it. Kitty froze; closed her eyes, "Please God. Please God." Peeking out of one eye, she looked over at the house. It was as quiet and formidable as a moment ago. She slid into the driver's seat, popped-open the glove box and pulled out a fresh pack of cigarettes. Taking a long drag, she settled back and watched the house. Kitty didn't want go back in there. She adjusted the rearview mirror and wiped at the smudged mascara around her eyes. Her face was pale, puffy and hungry. "Jesus," she mumbled and turned the mirror away. She would rather not see.

# Burnt Prairie

Isaac was tucked away from the crisp Colorado winds of early March. He was snug in bed with Summer, the long-haired blonde from the caves. Sure, she lived in a cave with a commune of hippies, which really seemed like an exotic term for the drugged homeless to Isaac, but she was beautiful and initially interesting. When Isaac first met her, he'd been in the Flat Irons on a geology assignment. She was clearly malnourished and tranquilized, but she moved like a butterfly, floating towards him and away all at once. Isaac knew he should keep his distance. ***She's probably got fleas,***  he told himself. Then Summer invited him to a cave party; he said it was purely an act of anthropological study. Summer had since become a frequent visitor to Isaac's bed, predominately when she was hungry.

Summer was hungry for pancakes this morning. She had curled into Isaac's chest; playing with the scattered hairs about his right nipple, a knock came as the door opened.

"Cohen, you got a call. I think it's your mom."

"Shit."

"Aww, I think it's sweet," Summer said.

That cinched it; he'd have to go to the phone now. He walked down the hall, balling up his sweatshirt in front of him to try and cover the erection tenting in his briefs, instead of donning it to cover his skinny frame.

"Mom?"

"Oh, Isaac, Oh, Isaac," her voice cracked.

"What's wrong? Is Ruth, okay?"

"Yes," she replied with a honking blow of her nose. Isaac pulled the phone away from his ear.

"Mom, what is it?"

"Your sister is fine. She's in her room, crying. It's your father."

"What did he do?"

"He had a heart attack. Can you believe that? I told him not to eat all that fat. It's all that bacon he thinks he's sneaking at Lee's Diner. But I know. And I told him I'm telling the Rabbi, too."

"Wait a minute. He had a heart attack?"

"Yes, he's in hospital. I don't know what to do. I need you to come home, Isaac."

"I can't just come home. I have classes."

"Well, use your sick days. I need you here. Your father could die."

"I can leave tomorrow after classes."

"Tomorrow? Oh, that's just fine. I'll tell your father to hold on. Maybe I'll get him to agree to hang around if I fry him up some bacon. And what about Ruth? What is she supposed to do? A selfish father in the hospital. A selfish brother away at school."

\*\*\*

Isaac found himself pinned on his back in the trunk of his 1965 Chrysler Newport, beginning to panic. He was trapped in total darkness. Before his eyes could adjust, his instantaneous reaction was to scream for help. He kicked his feet and pounded with his fists. Then he fell silent. There was no one to hear, no one to help. Isaac became hypersensitive to every motion and noise of the highway. Each time a tractor-trailer roared past that Chrysler would shake from side to side. Shit. Shit. Shit.

He was just outside of Hays, Kansas, on Highway 70, changing a flat on the rear passenger side. *I could be eating pancakes with Summer. I could be doing any number of things with Summer. Instead, I'm freezing my balls off and changing a flat tire to appease my mother.* Isaac threw the flat and the jack into the trunk and slammed the trunk shut and hurried to get out of the cold and back in the car. He pulled out a cigarette and put it to his lips. With the unlit cigarette dangling from his lips, he jumped into the front seat and grasped at the keys to get the car started and light-up. There were no keys in the ignition. He swiped at the ignition twice and looked incredulous. He started patting down his pockets with fervent smacks and digging. The cigarette, limp between his thin lips, fell to the floor of the car. *I set the keys down in the trunk.* Isaac could feel his stomach churn.

Shit! He turned and looked behind him as if he could see through the black vinyl backseat and find the keys resting in the dark trunk. Isaac climbed into the backseat and pulled at the upper part of the backseat that released to open up to the trunk. He slid his underweight frame into the opening, held taut by tension. Isaac went headfirst into the dark. As soon as he got entirely into the trunk, the backseat, free of any weight, it sprang up and clamped shut.

*Fuck! I'm gonna die in here. I'm gonna get plowed by one of those trucks, and that will be the end of me. They won't even think to look for me in the trunk. I'll just be buried in this car in a junkyard. My parents will have a ...* Isaac heard his mother's nasally voice ringing in his head, "You're father had a heart attack." *Okay, okay, I've got to calm down. I've got to think about something else. What are my options? How am I going to get out of here?* Isaac was already in position with his feet towards the backseat, so he rocked back his legs as much as possible, and kicked at the backseat. Nothing. Isaac repeated that action, again and again, screaming out a string of obscenities (that even in his frustration and fear he was impressed with).

The backseat would not budge. Isaac made a new approach. He managed to move by small shifts of his ass in one direction and a wriggle of his shoulders in the other direction. He tried to position himself at more of an angle so he'd have room to stretch out. Simultaneously, Isaac wondered how long he'd been in the trunk. He wondered how long he could breathe. He blamed his father. *Damn it, I wouldn't be in this stupid trunk if it weren't for him.*

***

Myron Cohen never needed anything but attention. He was a successful accountant, he was married with a son and daughter, and he had a deep laugh. Myron reveled in the fame of his name, even if it was not his own fame. The family always had hard-to-get table reservations and box office tickets. You didn't have to be a big celebrity or a real celebrity to get star treatment in St. Louis. The mere fact that Myron shared a famous name with the comedian that had played on

Ed Sullivan was all it took, and he got a big laugh out of it. It didn't hurt that Myron had the personality to pull it off. He was the opposite of Isaac in every way. Isaac was more like his mother: large slender pale hands preferred one-to-one conversation and desired more control over life. Whenever Myron was taking the family to a social event, Isaac and his mother faded to the background. But Ruthie, the unplanned and pleasant surprise child, rose to the occasion with their father.

Isaac had been 10 when Ruthie was born. He was uninterested and unimpressed, except for the fuss that came with her. His mother no longer had time for him, except to complain about how dirty and noisy he was all the time. His father was interested in Ruthie as a new addition to his act. ***Ladies and Gentlemen, look at the man in the gray suit with the pink frilly thing in his arms,*** Isaac could hear intoned in his head.

With the addition of Ruthie, Isaac felt his father's limelight seeking behavior transition from an annoying quality to a circus. Isaac started spending more time with his friends, and when he was at home more time, with his science books and the Torah. As his bar mitzvah approached, things took an unexpected turn. Myron developed a renewed interest in Isaac and the synagogue. The Cohen's always attended synagogue, always welcomed the Sabbath queen, and always held Seder. Growing up, Isaac had felt these activities were more about his father socializing with the Rabbi or showing off his Hebrew in front of a gentile client invited to Seder. It seemed like a business practice more than a faith. Isaac resented the sudden interest. His father was horning in on his moment. He was now 12, and he felt his father was horning in on the upcoming Bah Mitzvah.

***

*The air is getting thicker, clogging my throat, or is it my imagination.* Isaac shifted his weight and kicked at the backseat again, more in rage than the hope it would open. The car rocked from side to side as another tractor-trailer passed on the highway, followed by yet another. The Newport, with Isaac in it, was rushed by the velocity of tractor-trailers trying to make good time on the flat roads of Kansas. *I'll be damned if this car is going to be my coffin. My only other option is the trunk lock.* The tire was between Isaac and the trunk latch. He crawled backward on his back till his body was tight against the flat tire. His hands were sweating as his long fingers felt for the Starlock on the trunk. Yes, there it is. If I just turn, it should... The spring-loaded trunk popped right open. Isaac climbed out; he grabbed the car keys and shut the trunk on two hours of hell.

He clasped his hands to his clammy face and tried to take a deep breath, but a strong wind whipped across his face. According to the morning forecast, that wind was the precursor to the ice storm expected to roll in within the next couple of hours.

Back on the road, Isaac lit-up two cigarettes at once and then popped in his Elton John Eight Track to lighten his mood. The used green Newport had been a high school graduation gift. The installed Eight Track was Myron's big Hanukkah surprise to Isaac his freshman year at Colorado U. Isaac loved both the Eight Track and the Newport but felt these gifts were ties, strings that bound him to his father. The lighter popped on the dash, and Isaac lit-up, his third filtered Silk, Cut as **Goodbye Yellow Brick Road** drifted from the speakers. "When are you gonna come down, When are you going to land," Isaac sang along and his mood began to thaw.

\*\*\*

The Eight Track player had been installed by a friend of Myron's. It took the guy five hours and a lot of sweat. Isaac watched, squeamish about the sweat dripping off the fat man's hands, face, and hairy back as the guy squirmed under the dash, lodged between the vinyl seats and the floor.

"Say, Vince, can I help you out there," Myron said sitting on a bar stool in the man's garage.

"Yeah, have your son there get some beers out of the fridge."

Myron pointed to the olive refrigerator in the

corner of the garage and gave Isaac a wink, "Go ahead and get three, son."

Isaac opened the refrigerator to find it tightly packed with 12 oz. bottles of Busch Bavarian beer. He pulled out three beers and crossed quickly back to his car to watch the progress Mr. Michi was making on the Eight Track player.

"Here's your beer, Mr. Michi."

Vince slid his hairy, sweaty back out from under the dash and pulled himself up into the driver's seat.

Isaac winced, "Ah, don't you think it would be cooler outside the car. Maybe?"

"Isaac, when you get to be my age with my belly, you like to stay put."

Keeping his cigar in his mouth, Vince twisted open the beer barehanded. It frothed a little onto his hairy, sweaty chest, and he took a long swig.

"So, ah, how much longer do you think this is going to be?" Isaac asked, still holding his unopened beer.

"Let the man rest, son. Take a drink of that beer. It'll settle you down."

Isaac looked down at the beer. He was used to drinking beer. He drank every weekend with the guys, not his dad. Myron handed him a bottle opener from the tool bench. Isaac took a long slug and looked askance at Myron.

"I won't tell your mother."

Vince guffawed, and the ash on the cigar shook off onto the seat. Isaac wanted to dive in and brush it off, but he didn't want to get that close to Mr. Michi. And he didn't want to make the man angry. This guy was some kind of friend of his dad's, and the Eight Track player wasn't installed yet.

"So, when is Hanukah?" Vince asked.

"It's around Christmas time. It moves, but it's around Christmas," Myron said perched on that stool, leaning his lower back against Vince's grimy tool bench, looking fresh and clean as always. Even the heat of July couldn't ruffle Myron Cohen.

"I thought you said this was the boy's Hanukkah gift?" Vince said, reaching his already empty beer out to Isaac. Isaac took it.

"It is," Myron said.

"Kinda early, huh? I guess it's Hanukkah in July." Vince said and ruptured into laughter.

When Vince finished the installation, Isaac handed the keys to Myron. As they slid into the front seat, Myron said, "Is one beer too much for you, son?"

"No, I want to check the upholstery for cigar burns. Man, it stinks in here now."

"Just roll the windows down. It will fly right out. And not a word to your mother."

"I know, Dad."

"I mean about the beer and Vince. He's not a friend I'd have over to the house."

Isaac looked up from his meticulous fingering of the black vinyl. "Yeah, Dad, sure," he said and doubled over to inspect the floor mats.

\*\*\*

The headlights beamed out over a flat, snowy Kansas highway. The intense heat pumping from the dash was like a blanket, and it wrapped Isaac in a drowsy stupor. His hands loosened about the steering wheel, and the car drifted to the shoulder. Isaac jerked. I need to get some coffee.

Peering along the shoulder of the road for a sign promising coffee, warmth, and people, Isaac saw a dark lumbering shape. He slowed the car as he pulled over. The bulky frame of a man turned to face the headlights. Isaac leaned across the seat and rolled down the window.

"You okay, man?"

"I could really use a ride, you know?"

"Yeah, man, come on. I could use someone to keep me awake," Isaac said, opening the passenger door. A duffle bag landed with a thud in the back seat, and the door slammed shut. Isaac pulled back onto the highway.

"What's your name?"

"Steve." he said, rubbing his grime-stained hands together under the vent on the dash.

"It's kind of a cold night to be wandering a Kansas highway."

"Yeah, colder than a witch's tit out there."

"So, where are you headed?" Isaac asked.

"Kansas City."

Steve kept Isaac awake by telling stories about how tough he was. Isaac listened to tales of martial arts and bar fights. Steve always came out the winner.

"Let me give you the skinny. Guys like me are real mean sons-of-bitches."

"Yeah."

"What about you, man?"

"I was a Golden Gloves Champion, you know."

***What the hell have I picked up?*** In reality, Isaac had never thrown a punch. But he'd watched a lot of fights on Saturday night with Myron. The best he could do now was to try to believe his own lie. There was a light ahead. It was a truck stop. Perfect, I can get some coffee and get rid of this guy. He pulled into the truck stop.

"I need some coffee,"

"Yeah, me, too. You got any bread."

"Ah, here's two dollars. That's all I got. You go ahead. I gotta make a phone call."

"You wouldn't be calling Smokey?" Steve laughed.

"Nah, my girl. I gotta call my girl," he called over his shoulder as he dialed home.

***

Two years ago, Isaac was forced into taking Rebecca Rubenstein, a family friend, to her Prom. He had just walked into the kitchen looking for a nosh.

"What is that?" Isaac said point to the cleaner's bag draped across the kitchen table.

"That's your tuxedo for the prom," his mother sang in giddy glee. "Just back from the cleaners."

"It's red. And I'm not going to Prom."

"No, it's burgundy."

"If I were going, I would want powder blue with a ruffled shirt like Dan's."

"No you don't. Do you know what one of those things costs? Believe me, that look will go out of style, and years from now, you will know that your mother was right and be glad for this lovely burgundy tuxedo."

Isaac sighed.

"Where did you get it?" he said as he reached his hand cautiously under the plastic wrap of the cleaners to touch the velvet trim.

"Aunt Ruth. Your cousin Simon wore it to his Prom."

"That's not going to fit," he said, pulling back his hand, his voice cracking in complaint.

"He's two years older than you. Of course, it will fit."

This had been an ongoing problem for Isaac. In the mind of his mother, size had to do with age and not personal growth rates. He was always getting stuck with clothes too small from Simon.

"Here try it on."

"No."

"Try it on, Isaac," she said through her tall, coffee-stained teeth. Giving him a look that said she couldn't understand why he was ruining this joyful moment for her.

Isaac stomped to his room and stomped back with his large slender palms splayed out in an emphatic gesture to demonstrate his point. The pants were three inches too short. She smiled as if he had just proven her right. Isaac was aghast.

"Come on, we got time. Can't we get something else? Anything else?"

"We do not have time. You are wearing that this Friday when you take Rebecca Rubenstein to the Prom."

Rebecca was a stick of a girl with no chest and hairy arms. In the photo, her yellow-ruffled prom dress and her rhinestone glasses swallowed her small frame and bird-like face. Isaac took some solace in the fact that she came off second best in the photo. Rebecca had a dour expression. Isaac looked only slightly better because he was smiling. He was afraid if he didn't smile that his mother would call for a do-over.

***

***I'm stuck with this putz in my car, now I have to get to Indiana, tonight!***

Back on the road with the coffee and a Zagnut bar, Isaac was still trying to think of a way to lose this guy with the scraggly misshapen beard and bushy hair.

"Hey, do you want me to drive?" Steve said as he cracked open a Watney's Red.

"That's okay."

"You sure, man?"

"Yeah."

"Wanna Red Hot?" Steve said as he shook the box towards Isaac's face.

"No. So, what's with the army jacket, were you over in Vietnam?"

"I don't talk about it."

"So, there's a story behind the jacket."

"There's nothing. I don't talk about it. It's just a jacket."

Isaac was concentrating on the road covered with wide patches of ice. His mind kept drifting back to the jacket. He wanted to get a good look at the name on it, but it was too dark. Just then, Steve stretched out his arms and grabbed the back of Isaac's neck. Isaac threw his cup of hot coffee in Steve's face. Steve clutched his face. Isaac clutched the wheel.

"What the fuck?"

"What the fuck, me? Why are you grabbing my neck, you bastard."

"I was just trying to give you a rub. You looked tired."

"Well, I'm awake now, shit. And keep your damn hands to yourself," Isaac said. Steve reached down to his boot.

"Get your hands back up here. You pull anything out of that boot, and I'll kill us both," Isaac said, his hands tightening on the steering wheel.

Steve looked out at the icy highway, sat back in the seat, and remained quiet. Kansas City came and went. Steve decided to stay on till St. Louis. Upon entering St. Louis, Isaac drove to the downtown bus station and insisted Steve get out. This time there was no argument. Isaac pulled out of the parking lot with the doors locked. He sat at a flashing red light. It was the middle of the night. The next stop was home.

Isaac drove on to a gas station in Illinois and filled the tank at 40 cents a gallon. Then he headed out to U.S.I. He drove with the windows down to keep awake. With the diminutive show of morning light, Isaac pulled off the shoulder into a field filled with oil drills. He had to get a few necessary winks. He was falling asleep at the wheel. The pumps were bobbing in a peaceful rhythm that didn't exist in Isaac's life. He envied the mechanical, slow, purpose of the pumps. Oil was 40 cents a gallon, graduation was two years off, his plans of becoming anyone seemed like a kid's dream. He was tired. He wanted to feel grounded, well-grounded. He tried to remember the last time he really felt sure of himself and where he was going.

He nodded off and dreamt of his Bar Mitzvah when he'd wanted to feel Kavannah. He wanted to be imbued with holiness as he took his place in tradition. Perhaps, I'll be a Rabbi, he had thought in the days leading up to his Bar Mitzvah. But on his day, at his Bar Mitzvah reception, he felt second to his father, again. Myron had led Isaac around by the wrist to every man in the room.

"Look at this, a real man's watch. A Bulova Accutron Spaceview Model H watch! Isn't that something! The tuning fork divides every second into 360 equal parts!" Myron said over and over again.

Isaac could still hear him as he was starting to wake, and he still didn't know what it meant. He looked down at the silver Bulova, keeping time, effortlessly, perfectly pumping out every second. He could hear his father in that crowded room at the Ritz.

"That's my son. He's a smart one, not like his old man. He's got real genius," Myron had said to the Rabbi. Isaac heard it. He sought his father out to tell him, what? Isaac didn't know, but he knew he wanted to be near his dad. He heard his father's low chuckle from the back of the coatroom. Isaac pushed through the overcoats and fur coats. There he was. "Helping the coat check girl," Myron had said later. There he was with his hand up her skirt and his face nestled in her blond hair.

Isaac rubbed his face, then looked down at his watch. It was nearly 5a.m. His mom was waiting. His dad was waiting. If only he could stay here in the long, burnt-yellowed grass prairie, under the faint odor of sulfur, under a fading sky of destinies, then perhaps he could pluck a direction from that veil above or plumb the earth for substance, for more than this life of illusions. He wanted to stay, but he had to go.

# I Heart Burt

     I am both partial to and particular about angora sweaters. I like to wear them without a bra. I imagine that is what it would feel like to press my breasts against a hairy chest. I am obsessed with hairy chested men, and it all started with Burt Reynolds in Cannonball Run. I was 9 when I saw the movie on TV one Saturday afternoon. I've been a Reynolds, and hairy chest fanatic ever since. Even when I go out dancing with the girls, I go braless in my angora. Once I braved going braless to work. While I found it liberating, it was also distracting.

     A little tip, I also have a thing for hairy hands. Hair on the outset side of the hands with hairy knuckles is a good sign that they would have a hairy chest, but all too often they turn out to be shavers. The worst are men with minuscule hairy chests. The kind with just a little cluster in the middle or the rings around the nipples. I try to get their shirts off early in the game, so I can call it quits before the guy gets too hot. I don't even really get started myself until I see that carpet of chest hair. With today's trends, I rarely meet a man up to my standards. Recently, I started going for foreigners, immune yet to our American hairless ways. But my heart always remains loyal to Burt Reynolds.

    I live with my cat Moliere and my tenacious companion, Bipolar Depression. I am medicated, but there is no cure. When I lost my job at the public library due to federal cutbacks, it triggered a depression that left me near comatose on the couch. I ate take out every meal that I bothered to eat, and my garbage piled up until mice appeared. Moliere proved to be a fair mouse catcher. When the depression sets-in, I feel like I am made of paper, an origami Emily. I can be so easily torn. I also wonder things like what would happen if you actually put a butter knife in the toaster. How bad would the jolt be? When my mood shifted, I went out and bought 42 loaves of bread to make toast for everyone in my complex. I informed all of my neighbors that they were welcome, and to eat the buttered raisin toast while it was still warm, for it was best that way. When the landlord came to my door, I invited him in for toast and coffee. I no longer felt like I was made of paper, but a glowing light that could not be doused even in the darkest night. Others thought I really needed a new job. And I did land a new job as a librarian at Washington University's Law Library. I am wonderful in my new position, of course, because I am painstakingly precise and efficient (except when depressed). There are long periods between the mood swings, and while this is fortunate on the one hand, it adds to a certain level of denial. But for now, I just sweep the hairless lovers and the hairy ones under the rug of a free spirit. And only Moliere has witnessed my howling anger as I brake dishes in the kitchen or sleep in the drained bathtub.

I have a fantasy hairy boyfriend. One night imagined him tickling me while I was chewing gum, and it fell out of my mouth and landed in his chest hair. We tried peanut butter, which made a mess. We tried ice, which aroused him. In the end, I had to shave a small patch to remove the gum. I hated that bare patch and tried to avoid it during sex. Then I realized if I did press a breast against that smooth spot, it felt like cheating on him and in a rather exciting way.

In reality, I had to try to remove my gum from Moliere. Have you ever got gum stuck in a black cat?

It is exhausting going through the mood swings, but the worst part is the lack of understanding and compassion in our culture. I'm not asking for a lot here, just don't fear me and call me crazy. Isolation is not suitable for someone like me, we need a support group. But that is hard to find. Maybe they could just open a

Crazies R Us, and we could support each other. Of course, two manic people or depressed people together usually does not bode well. It gets a lot worse than excessive take out or toast production.

We had this alcoholic at the library, he snuck sips from the flask in his jacket and fell asleep in the stacks. He was probably homeless, but he dressed nicely, and he was hairy. During a Manic phase, I found myself spending a lot of time having sex in the stacks with the drunk. I got bored of him, as will happen during a manic state, so I decided to take him into a swinger's bar I found online and trade-up. I found one couple interested in me, but not him. So, I dumped him and went home with Audra and Kevin. Kevin wasn't really my type, hairless, but Audra was something new. New has a short lifespan in Mania, and that lasted just a month or more. And then I was back in a full-blown depression and disgusted with myself. I pulled on an angora sweater over my bare breasts and crawled into bed. Again, I felt like that shell of a paper Emily but unfolded and torn, and I was angry with Burt Reynolds. I cried myself to sleep in a sweater that scratched and inflamed.

# Man in Black

Orange Sherbet reminds me of my summer with Johnny Cash. I was eleven years old; my brother Marcus was seven. We were spending the summer with Dad. Well, not the entire summer, three weeks. That year Dad had negotiated Mom down from five weeks. When I asked why Marcus and I had to go at all, she said, "Look, Gemma, I need a break. Your father could do something." That summer, Dad did something in August.

"Listen, kids, I have to go to work. I'll try and get out early. Your leftovers from McDonald's are in the fridge, and there's soup in the pantry."

I stared into my bowl of Captain Crunch. Five golden mush lumps floated in the milk. I didn't want to look up or open my mouth, afraid I'd give voice to the lump in my throat. I didn't want to make Dad feel bad, but I didn't want to spend another day locked-up in the A/C in an unfamiliar apartment.

"Ok, here's a five. Get yourself some ice cream if the ice cream truck comes by. And we'll go out for dinner tonight. Okay? Okay."

Marcus and I continued to sit at the Formica table that used to be in Grandma Shirley's basement. A lot of the furniture in Dad's new apartment migrated from different rooms of Grandma Shirley's house. I had the vinyl seat with the duct tape down the middle.

When I hesitated sitting in that chair on our first morning, Dad had said, "It's kitschy." I didn't know what that was, but I didn't believe him. "Be good," Dad called as he walked out the backdoor with his computer bag in one hand and his tie in the other. We listened for the shut of the car door, the start of the engine, and the fade of supervision.

"At least Mom kisses us good-bye," Marcus said, setting his bowl in the sink. "And gets us a sitter." The phone rang.

"What are we going to do, Gemma?" Marcus said.

The phone rang again. I picked it up from the base on the kitchen wall.

"Hello?"

"Gemma, watch out for your brother. Call me at work if you need anything. And don't go anywhere."

"Okay, Dad."

Was there anywhere *to go?* Marcus and I weren't familiar with this neighborhood. The entire block was squashed together with dark, red brick buildings, each three stories high, each with a green and red door. The sameness of this place was interrupted with the occasional empty lot of weeds. But in the lot to the left of our building was a big garden, more like a collection of little gardens. At night, from our bedroom window, I could see the outlines of towering sunflowers and shadowy patches in the moonlight. During the day, it was a tangle of green with moments of color. St. Louis sure was different from home. Last summer, Dad still lived back home in Atlanta. We stayed with him in a Condo in the city; that was when he was dating Heather, who looked at Marcus and me like we were cockroaches on her kitchen floor. I added my bowl to the climbing tower in the sink. Heather would hate this place.

"What did he want?" Marcus said.

"Nothing."

Marcus sat on the floor, watching Tom and Jerry cartoons and biting his toenails.

"Mom doesn't like that."

"At least dad has cable, so we can watch cartoons all day. The last place had cable, too."

"Stop biting your toenails. Mom doesn't like it."

"Mom's not here," Marcus said, straining to jam a new toe between his teeth." He spits the ripped nail on the floor. "Do you think we could get Mom to get cable?"

"No. It's too expensive."

"Hmm, maybe that's why Dad lives in this crummy place to pay for the cable."

"You're gonna have stinky feet breath."

By afternoon, I was tired of cartoons and felt stiff from the A/C. I wanted to go out in the sun, in the garden.

"Want some ice cream?"

"Do you hear the ice cream man?" Marcus said as he jumped up and looked out the window.

"No, but I'm sick of sitting in here. Let's check out that garden."

We weren't outside but 10 minutes, and I already missed the air conditioning.

"Huh, it's a vegetable garden," Marcus said. He nudged at some swollen eggplant near his untied, dingy converse. "I think Mom tries to get me to eat this stuff."

Each garden patch was different. Some were vegetables, some flowers, and a ton of leafy or stalk-like plants that I didn't know. There were butterflies and bees, both real and ornamental, little stools, ceramic bunnies, and chimes.

"This is really boring, and it's getting hot, Gemma."

"Do you think one of these belongs to Dad?"

"I'm going inside. If the ice cream man comes, I want a bomb pop."

I continued to make my way through the plots until I found a shady place inside a little vine-constructed tee-pee. The ground was damp in this plot.

It must have just been watered. I decided to squat so as not to get my white shorts dirty. Dad didn't do laundry too often. I found a little stick and began to dig my initials in the cool, packed soil of the tee-pee. I wonder why someone made a tee-pee of vines. I ran my finger over the long green tendrils to see if I could identify the plant. I'd just finished Ms. Seibert's 5th grade honors Science that year. I felt a long, curvy, bumpy pod. I plucked the green bean. It was the longest, thinnest green bean I'd ever seen. I could make a necklace out of this, but a green bean bracelet would be much cooler.

The urgent clang of the ice cream man brought back the heat of the afternoon. I dashed from the green bean teepee and tripped over the red-painted railroad tie framing the garden patch. I hit dry, hard earth catching myself with my right knee, palms, and chin. The clamor of the bell, along with the circus music, sounded about half a block away. I got up, brushed my burning, grass patterned palms on my t-shirt, and ran through the maze of mini-gardens. The clamor of other kids hailing the ice cream man rose over the leafy labyrinth. I hit the open expanse of lawn in front of the community garden. I could see two older girls and a boy walking away with their frozen delights. The churning circus tones called out, and I arrived at the front walk. I tried to make a quick study of the truck's offerings. What do I want? My heart was pounding, and I was beginning to feel the pain in my chin. My eyes scanned up and down the pictures of ice cream and popsicles.

"Hey, kid! It's your turn. What do you want?"
"Ah, um. A Bomb Pop and a Push-Up."
"That's $2.50."

As soon as he said it, I realized I'd left the $5 bill on the kitchen table.

"Wait! I left my money inside."
"I can't wait, kid," and he started to turn up the volume of the circus music.

"Wait! I have money here." I pulled two crumpled dollars from my pocket.

"Well, which one do you want?"
"I want the Bomb Pop and a Push-Up."
"Kid, you don't got enough. Which one? The Bomb Pop or the Push-Up?"

I looked back at the apartment. I could see Marcus at the window waving to me.

"The Bomb Pop," I said, looking down at the mud squished between my toes and smeared across the weave of my sandal on my right foot.

"And I think I'll take two Push-Ups," a voice boomed behind me.

I looked up, and standing next to me was a broad-shouldered man in black leather.

"Hey, kid. Your bomb pop?" the ice cream man said.

I took the oversized Popsicle and my change from the ice cream man, but I looked at the man with the swept-back, black hair, and large sideburns. He looks hot. That's probably why he wants two Push-Ups. I started towards the apartment to give Marcus his Bomb Pop. The noise of the ice cream truck resumed as it pulled from the curb.

"Miss?"

I turned around and just looked at him.

"Miss? Do you want one of these Push-Ups? I can't eat two. I gotta watch my figure."

"I don't know you."

"Very wise of you. I'm Johnny Cash. I'm your neighbor, too." And he gestured to the floor beneath our apartment. By this time, Marcus had come out to fetch his Bomb Pop. I took the Push Up.

"I saw you in the garden. I don't think your Dad has a plot. Would you like to see mine?"

"Is it just more vegetables?" Marcus asked with blue juice already dribbling from his chin.

"Is it the tee-pee?"

"No. It's better. It's behind Mrs. Hardy's sunflowers."

Johnny Cash gestured, and we followed. He was right, his was better.

"That's awesome," Marcus said. "Can I sit on it?"

Johnny Cash's garden was a moss-molded sofa and a moss-covered tree stump for a coffee table with potted flowers on it.

"Sure."

The three of us sat on the moss sofa. I was in the middle. It was cooler in this shady spot, and there was a soft breeze.

"Miss? How do you open this thing?"

"Oh. You peel the top off, and then as you eat it, you Push Up with the handle. Oh, and thanks." I brushed my long blond hair away from my face. "It's kinda windy."

"It feels good, and you're welcome. It's hard being a kid on a hot day. It's hard being Johnny Cash on a hot day."

"Who's that?" Marcus asked. He was leaning around me and dripped more blue juice, but this time he dripped it on my shorts and my left leg. The sticky blue syrup ran down my pale thigh, turning pink in the sun.

"Me, of course. Good pick, miss. Johnny Cash loves orange sherbet."

"Really? It's my favorite." I wiped at my leg with the palm of my hand.

"Why do you talk like that?" Marcus blurted, leaning across me this time.

"Marcus," I said through my teeth.

"Like what?"

"You call yourself by your name like Elmo."

"Is that a friend of yours, Marcus?"

"Nah. He's on Sesame Street," I said.

"Oh. Well, I just like being Johnny Cash, I

guess."

"I like being Gemma. That's my name."

"That's a beautiful name."

"Thanks. My Dad picked it."

"I call her Germma because girls are gross," said Marcus. His dark curls were sticking to his forehead with sweat. Everything about him was sticky.

I went into the garden every day that week and ordered Push-Ups every time the ice cream man passed-by. I was prepared with the money in my pocket. And I made sure I always had enough for a Push Up for Johnny Cash, too. But I didn't bump into Mr. Cash again. So, I wound up eating twice as much orange sherbet.

When we watched cartoons in the afternoon, I would hear his shower run and his muffled singing. I tried to make out the lyrics. Although I didn't recognize any of his songs, I liked to hear him sing. I'd press my ear to the cool hardwood floor and make up my own words as I listened.

"Gemma, get off that floor," Dad said. "Come on, she's going to be here any minute.

"So?"

"So, get over here and act like a lady, not a baby on the floor."

"I'm not a baby. I'm listening to Johnny Cash."

"What? Since when do you listen to Johnny Cash?"

"Since I met him in the garden."

"Excuse me?"

"He bought her an ice cream because there was only money for one, and I got it," Marcus chimed in.

"You are not supposed to talk to strangers for one. You are not supposed to accept things from strangers for two. And why do you think this stranger is Johnny Cash?"

"Because that's his name, and he lives downstairs."

"Oh. Oh, yeah, right. The impersonator."

"What?" Marcus said, wrinkling his nose.

"Kids, he impersonates Johnny Cash at the Hard Rock Café downtown."

"You know where he works? What does he do?" I said.

"He sings."

"Can we hear him sing? Please?"

"Maybe, if it will keep you off the floor."

With that, there was a knock at the backdoor, and within the hour, Marcus and I were pretty much invisible. Dad made us go to bed early that night, too. He said it was grown-up time for him and his friend Tanya. Marcus and I brushed our teeth and climbed into the double bed in our room.

"I get the window side."

"Not fair! You take the window side every night, Gemma!"

"No fighting in there," Dad hollered.

"Fine," I hissed and threw a pillow at him.

Sometime in the night, I woke up, I mean wide awake. I wasn't use to going to bed so early. My body just wasn't tired anymore. I lay in the graying light listening to Marcus snore softly. I watched his face. His mouth was hanging open enough for me to see his two oversized front teeth. I was wondering what he would look like if he were a rabbit when I heard something. It sounded like a grunt, like if someone got punched in the stomach. I heard it again.

"Marcus, Marcus," I whispered, tugging the elbow of his sleeve.

"Wha?"

"Do you hear that?"

"No. I'm sleeping," he said. "Why? What was it?" He pulled the blankets up to his chin; just then, I heard it again.

"Wait, I'm coming with you," Marcus said as he stood closer to me than normal. He stood next to me like I was Mom or something. I cracked open the door and peered into the blackness of Dad's room. Marcus peeked over my shoulder. Even though I was older, he was nearly as tall as me. We got down and crawled into the entrance to Dad's bedroom. Scrunched together on the floor, we watched. We watched I didn't know what, but I did. I just had never seen it before. I never thought about what it looked like, but I didn't think it would look like that. It was so rough. In silence, we crawled back to bed.

"What were they doing?" he asked.

"Didn't Mom ever talk to you about it?"

"About what? Naked wrestling? No."

"About making babies," I said angrily. I felt like I was going to cry.

"Is that what they're doing? Dad wants another baby?"

"Go to sleep, Marcus."

I tried to sleep, but I couldn't. I couldn't get comfortable. I felt funny being so close to Marcus. I felt funny thinking at all. I wanted to go home. I wanted my Mom. I had to get away from the apartment, from that moment. Anger was twisting and coiling in my stomach. Without shoes, once all was quiet, I slipped down the hall and out the back door. The Sun was starting to come up; the gray light was warming to a fine yellow. The dew dolloped grass tickled and licked my feet as I made my way to Johnny Cash's living room. I sat on the sod sofa, not caring if my nightgown got muddy, feeling like I might puke. And that's when I saw him park his old Buick.

He didn't seem surprised to see me there, and I hadn't even realized I was crying till he offered me a white handkerchief.

"May I have a seat?" he said as he sat down.

He was in all black again with that same leather jacket. I took the handkerchief from him. It was embroidered with JC in the corner in black, and I noticed he had a big gold ring on almost every finger.

"Gemma, what are you doing out here?"

"You're a liar," jumped from my lips. "You're a liar. You're not Johnny Cash. He's dead. I know. I looked it up on Google. I'm not some dumb, little kid, you know."

"I don't think you're dumb, Gemma. And I'm sorry. I was just pretending."

"Pretending is lying. Grown-ups are always lying."

"I think pretending is fun. Don't you pretend?"

"Not anymore," I mumbled into my shoulder.

"Aww, I hate to hear that. I really do." I wanted to scoot closer to him, to curl up in his lap like I use to with Dad. I wanted him to hold me. Instead, I closed my eyes, waiting for his warm, deep voice.

"Gemma, let me tell you something. Grown-ups are just big, ugly children. And sometimes we pretend because we don't know what else to do."

"I don't think I like growing-up," I said, opening my eyes and gazing out at the breaking light.

"Then, don't stop dreaming, Gemma."

I blew my nose in the handkerchief.

"I didn't know men wore rings."

"Sure. What about wedding rings?"

"My Dad never wore one."

"Well, every man is different. Look at me. I like a lot of rings and sod sofas."

"You're funny."

"Thanks. Pretty sunrise, isn't it? I love a good sunrise."

"Yeah. Yeah. Me too," I said, although I didn't remember ever paying much attention before.

We watched the sun come all the way up, the soft yellow and pink blushing into day. Johnny Cash walked me to my backdoor, where we met Dad and Tanya kissing in the door jamb. At first, Dad looked like Marcus when he'd been caught doing something Mom didn't like, but then he looked like he couldn't figure out the answer to a really hard math problem.

"Gemma? What the hell are you doing outside?"

"I, I..."

I looked back from his face to her face. They both seem surprised or scared, just like me.

"I'm gonna go," Tanya said as she bent like a flamingo and jammed a foot in one of her high-heels. She gave Dad a kiss on his cheek that he didn't seem to notice, and she squeezed past Johnny Cash and me.

"Good night, ma'am," said Johnny Cash with a nod of his head.

"What the hell are you doing with my daughter?"

"She was sleepwalking, Andy. I found her in the garden when I got home from work and went to water my flowers. Early morning is the best time to water them, you know. She may still be asleep. It's best not to wake them," Johnny Cash said.

Everyone stood there. We just stood there. Dad looked guilty. I was trying hard not to blush, not to remember what I'd seen. I didn't want Dad to touch me.

"I gotta get her in bed. I'll talk to you later," Dad said, steering me by my shoulders into the apartment. He shut the kitchen door behind him. I could see the back of Johnny Cash's head-turning away.

"Gemma, I don't believe you were sleepwalking."

"I wasn't."

"Then what were you doing with Johnny Cash?"

I stared at my wet toes. There was a grass clipping on the right pinky.

"Did he hurt you?"

"No."

"Are you sure? Cause I'll…"

"No, no. It's not like that."

"Like what?"

"I know about safe touch and bad touch, Dad. They've talked to us about it in school since first grade. Even Marcus knows about that."

"Well, then what were you doing out there?"

"I went for a walk. He saw me in his garden when he got home."

"Gemma, why would you go for a walk at night?"

"Tanya."

"Ah, ah, what about Tanya?"

"I heard you. We saw you, okay," I turned my back to him and gripped the back of the kitchen chair in front of me.

"Oh, we were just…"

"I'm not a baby, Dad. I know what you were doing."

"I'm sorry, Gemma. Next time I'll remember to close the door."

"Next time?"

"Okay, sorry. No next time, for now. Gemma? Do you have...are you...I don't know what to say."

"I'm tired."

"Okay, go to bed."

I let go of the chair, my fingernails had pressed little crescent moons into the vinyl. As I stepped into the hall, Dad asked me, "Gemma, let's not tell Mom about this, okay?"

"Yeah," I said, and I felt empty inside, in my chest. I didn't know if I was telling him the truth at that moment and, for the first time in my life, I didn't care if I was lying to my Dad.

He never asked me about the incident again. The following weekend, on our last night in town, Dad surprised Marcus and me with a trip to the Hard Rock Café to see Johnny Cash. I hadn't seen him since the night in the garden. I was so excited. I wore my favorite pink daisy sundress. We got a table right in the front, and Dad let us order whatever we wanted off the menu. It was great. I got a chocolate milkshake, cheeseburger, and fries. There were posters and photos everywhere.

The music was thunderous, and the waiters and waitresses were dressed really crazy. Dad said they were dressed like the 70s when he was born. It was really cool. I love that way back in the olden day stuff. But it was hard to concentrate on all the people or my dinner because I kept looking for Johnny Cash.

"Hey, Dad. Can I ask you a question?" Marcus said with a mouthful of fries.

"You just did."

"Ha, Ha, Ha. You're real funny, Dad."

"Well, what is it?"

"Whatever happened to that lady?"

"What lady?"

I shot a shut-up look at Marcus, so he just kept going.

"The one that came over. The one like Grandma Shirley."

"The one like Grandma Shirley?" Dad said, looking confused. "The only lady that came over was Tanya."

"Yeah. Her. What happened to her?"

"Marcus, how is Tanya like your Grandma Shirley?"

"She smells like cigarettes and too much perfume."

Just then, the lights went low, from the darkness emerged the strum of a guitar, and a spotlight came up on Mr. Johnny Cash. He sang all the songs I had listened to through the floorboards, but now I could really hear the lyrics and see him.

"Dad, quick, I need a pen."

"Why?"

"Come on."

"Okay, okay. We'll get one from the waitress."

I bounced my foot on the peg of my barstool and scratched at a mosquito bite on my calf as I listened and waited for the pen. Once the waitress returned with a pen I began jotting down lyrics on my paper napkin, the ones I couldn't understand before through the floor like "I keep my eyes wide open all the time, I keep the ends out for the tie that binds" from *I Walk The Line* and from *A Boy Named Sue* "And I came away with a different point of view. And I think about him, now and then, Every time I try and every time I win."

Everything was better than I had imagined. He stood there like a rock with his guitar. His jaws quivered when he sang, and he gave an occasional tilt into the microphone and then a wink just at me. At that moment, I belonged to something special. Johnny Cash broke into a *Ring of Fire*, and the restaurant erupted in applause. I was so proud. They didn't know him like I knew him. I watched their shadowed faces, eating, talking, and laughing. I looked at Marcus, stuffing his face with fries, Dad playing with his napkin, and singing along. I knew they saw a man on a dark stage, but I saw the man in black.

As the show ended, Dad reached across and handed me his napkin that he'd twisted into the shape of a rose. "For my lady," he said as the lights came up. Mr. Cash descended the stage and crossed to our table. He and Dad chatted for a while like neighbors, like I'd never seen at home. He shook Dad and Marcus' hands. When he bent down to hug me, I was swallowed by his black leather coat. He was warm. I could smell soap, and some men's cologne suffuse the air inside this leather cocoon. I felt heady, swaddled in dark security.

      Some people pretend to be a good parent while running away from home. Others pretend to be a celebrity while living a small life, working a small stage. I wanted to stay glued to that moment, wrapped inside that coat with him, but I knew I couldn't. I had to pretend to be innocent while life was forcing me to grow-up. I whispered into his chest, "I believe in you, Mr. Cash," and I let go.

# Swimming Middle River

I watched my granddaughter bobbing up and down in the blue water. Her wet, round cheeks buoyed the pink trimmed goggles, but they gave way to the slimming jawline. She was losing that rounded, cuddly look. Her features were being chiseled out with time: a pointy chin, a finely etched nose; soon angular cheekbones would appear and wash away that baby bloom, bringing with it the flush of pre-pubescent daring. Already Jenny's limbs were long and slender. I watched as the swim coach clasped Jenny's wrists between her forefingers and thumbs, pumping Jenny's arms in long sweeping arcs in the air, modeling the stroke she was expected to perfect in the water. Only 7, and already Jenny was competing against children 2 years her senior in swim competitions, already on her way to being a lifeguard. Not like me. I was an ugly swimmer, awkward and clumsy, making big splashes.

I had learned to swim with other children: my brothers Tommy and Paul; across the street, my best friend Phyllis Kalowski and kid brother Bernie. And the Cooper boys, Jimmy and Roy, who lived on the corner of the block, in the large yellow house. A whole gang of kids from St. Mary's parish, a brood of knees and elbows sloshing in Middle River like water buffalo, always moving in a herd, sweaty and looking for sugar and shade. Phyllis saddled with her younger brother Bernie, forever whining, was always taking the biggest dare just to shake him off, leave him behind. My brothers insisted on being paired-up and leaving me behind. The Cooper boys, Jimmy, large and slow, brought up the rear, cowing to his younger brother Roy's orders, a natural leader. Roy was in front and full of fun ideas. Jimmy lurked in the background, looking for his next hot foot victim or wedgie opportunity.

Paul, Tommy, and I were staying in St. Mary's Parish with our grandparents that summer. Mom was busy working as many hours as she could get just to keep us fed, clothed, and save a little. Plus, she insisted on us staying in a private school at St. Laborious, even with Dad gone for the next year. It was a countdown till he came back: a second paycheck, another problem. I don't think all my mom's tears were for missing him, not all the time. But that summer mom was working every shift she could get, saving every penny to get us out of the city and into a better life. Maybe, if Dad lived somewhere with new friends, he'd get into less trouble. So, while we were in St. Mary's parish with grandma and grandpa missing our mom to work and our dad to jail, we learned to swim in Middle River.

Middle river had some shallow banks, but it turned to a swift current after rain. You had to be careful, especially since we were just a bunch of kids goofing around and teaching ourselves to swim. There wasn't the luxury of adult supervision back then, nor swim teams and indoor pools. Swimming was mostly playing in the water to keep cool, because there wasn't any air conditioning, except at the movies. But we had fun. One day, I remember, Roy led us all through the water in follow the leader, but each person had to do a different kind of swim stroke. We had a blast. Tommy and Paul were the Mertwins and swam, sort of, with their legs entangled. I was a starfish, kind of splayed out and paddling my hands and feet to make movement. Phyllis was stuck on the bank with Bernie, the cry baby. Jimmy was a walrus and belly-flopped wherever he pleased. Roy was a shark, and he swam underwater with one hand sticking out above his head.

When we got waterlogged, we'd sit on the bank and dry off in the sun. We swam in our underwear and, partway through the summer, Phyllis would not strip down and swim every time; I thought she was turning into one of them finicky girls. It pissed me off. But on most days, we would lay on the bank waiting to dry so we could get dressed in our denim pants and cotton shirts or cotton dresses again. We would watch the clouds go by and pretend we saw different shapes in the blue sky, one was more outlandish than the next. But it felt good in the heat, beads of water drying slowly from our skin. Brushing away the sediment from our feet before we put our socks and shoes back on, and making plans for what to do next. It was Roy's idea that we pool our money together and split some penny candy. If one of us had been really good, they might have enough money to get ice cream, and we'd share it all around. However, the kid that gave up the big bounty got control of dolling out spoon time, which was never fair but based more on how much the kid liked you.

    I watched Jenny cut through the water like she was made for swimming, turning her headway out of the water, and taking a breath. Then it all came back to me: the kids, the water, and the fire. We'd all of us been at Phyllis and Bernie's house, hanging out in front of the new blue window fan at the back of the house. Tommy, Paul, Roy, and Jimmy had taken the chairs, so the rest of us lounged on the floor. It was still hot. The boys were getting restless. Tommy and Paul wanted to play ball. But Roy said it was too hot. So we settled on Middle River, which sent Bernie into tears. Phyllis had had enough and drug him upstairs and pushed him into his closet. We all followed to watch the show. Bernie didn't fight back. He just dropped to his bottom upon a pair of shoes and a baseball glove and continued to cry. Phyllis slammed the door. "Let's go swimming," she announced.

"He's just going to follow us and cry the whole way," Tommy said.

"No, he won't." Roy took a shim of wood meant to hold the bedroom door open and wedged it under the closet door, keeping Bernie shut-in.

"He's going to get hot in there. And what about when my mom gets home?"

"We'll come back before your mom is home from her factory shift," said Roy.

"Oh, well then, let's go," Phyllis said.

We started to file out, but I hung back for a bit. I felt terrible for Bernie. Jimmy had hung back too and was playing with a book of matches. I didn't want a hot foot, so I hightailed it out of there and caught up with the others.

We had three hours to make the half-hour walk to Middle River, swim, air dry, and walk back. Paul had a watch, so he was in charge of keeping the time. Once we got to Middle River, I was feeling better. It was good to have Phyllis in the water again. We played mermaids while the boys had some splashing game going.

Paul forgot about the time since the watch was in his shoe on the bank to keep it dry. We all had to pull on our sun-clothes over our wet underwear and run.

As we got closer to town, we heard the sirens.

We saw the billowing black smoke swallowing Phyllis' house. "Oh, my god! Bernie is in there."

"There isn't anyone in there miss, we checked," said a nearby firefighter.

"He's in the closet on the second floor," I said. And I looked at Jimmy, who was standing there smiling at the ground. Roy glanced back at Jimmy, too, with a nervous look. And I knew, Roy and Jimmy were the only other ones who knew for sure how that fire got started. Roy glanced back at the Fire Captain, then at a hysterical Phyllis. Tommy and Paul had taken up ranks in the rear, blank-faced.

Even after the funeral, Phyllis wouldn't talk to us or anyone. I knew she was blaming herself. And I wasn't speaking-up about Jimmy. At the wake, at the funeral, on the street, Jimmy would leer at me before raising one finger to his lips in a "shush" fashion. And I stayed quiet. I was afraid. I was 7, the age of reason, and reason told me Jimmy wasn't beyond killing again.

I watched as Jenny climbed from the pool. She stretched out and waved at me. My granddaughter was 7, the age of reason. How would she make sense of this tale of mine? I didn't tell anyone about Jimmy and Bernie, until my husband, when we were newlyweds. He comforted me and said I was just a child. I didn't know.

"But I didn't tell," I cried.

Jimmy went on to kill neighborhood cats, and he eventually went to the asylum. Roy was killed in

Vietnam. But nothing ever happened to me. What kind of person was I to hold on to such a secret? And that was the worst punishment of all, drowning in my silence.

# The Tooth of It

Linda called the Realtor, pretending to be an interested buyer of the Condo. Over the phone, she managed to flirt her way into an impromptu showing. Linda would have time for lunch before heading over, but she hated to eat alone. It was a reminder of how lonely she felt. She missed Tommy. The way he looked at her and held her. He rekindled something deep inside of Linda that had been gone so long. She had forgotten that she ever felt alive and beautiful.

It started off innocent just High school sweethearts bumping into each other at Starbucks nearly 50 years later. It was just a cup of coffee.

"Linda, Linda Norman?"

"Oh, my God. Tommy Bishop?"

"How have you been?" Tommy said. Simultaneously, he ran his hand through his thinning blonde hair.

"I'm good, but I'm Linda Pearson now," she said.

"Oh, of course, I remember," he said. "Is your husband here?" He looked about the shop as if he would know the man on sight.

"No, he's back home. I'm just taking a little vacation to see the family."

"Well, let me buy you a cup of coffee. Do you have time to catch-up?"

"That sounds wonderful. I drink an Almondmilk Honey Flat White."

"Is that even a coffee?" He chuckled and got in line.

Linda found a free table and brushed off the crumbs. She had planned on getting a Morning Bun but, just now, she didn't want any carbs. Over coffee, Tommy asked Linda if she'd been to the new restaurant on Main street. When she said no, he extended an invitation. Linda gladly accepted. It would be nice to get away from her sister-in-law Kristie's meatloaf.

In her Spanx, in front of the mirror, Linda held the only dress she packed up to her shoulders. It was a day dress. She needed an evening dress. Maybe Kristie would have something she could squeeze into.

"This would look nice for an evening dinner dress," Kristie said.

"Do you have something a little less conservative?"

"Yes, I've got this basic black dress,"

"Oh, I think, with the Spanx, I just might squeeze into it."

"Why do I get the feeling we are getting you ready to go on a date?" Kristie asked.

"Oh, he's an old boyfriend from 50 years ago. I just want to look my best. I don't want to look old and fat, even if I am."

As Linda put on her makeup, she felt like she was back in High School. The old feelings of promise, of expectation, had arrived right on cue as she prepared for another date with Tommy. Linda was sure to call home before she left. Brian, her middle son, was staying with his father. It had been Brian who suggested Linda take a short vacation from caring for Gary.

Tommy and Linda smiled and giggled more than was customary for their age. Both of them were lonely. Before dinner, Tommy took her on a nostalgic tour of the small town. They reminisced up and down Main street and over Benton High School campus.

"How long will you be in town?"

"I fly out Friday," she said. Her smile slackened.

"Let's make the most of it then," Tommy said. "So, what have you done all these years?"

"Just a housewife, and you?"

"I was an insurance salesman," he said.

"And you're not now?"

"I opted for early retirement," Tommy said.

"How nice," she said.

"Not really, I had to sell my business, what was left of it, to some younger kid in his thirties," he said.

"Had to?"

"I had some financial issues. I was visiting the casino more than my office. Actually, I was lucky there weren't any legal ramifications," he said. He looked down at his empty plate.

"I understand. Things don't turn out as we planned. Gary was diagnosed with Chrones 15 years ago. When something like that happens, you turn from wife to nurse. He wears a colostomy bag. I change it. And a year ago, he was diagnosed with early-onset Dementia," she said. "I'm sorry this is not dinner conversation."

"Why don't you get some help or put him in a home?

"A home is out of the question. It would drain all of our savings."

"How old is he?" Tommy asked.

"He's 7 years my senior. My mother tried to warn me. But I was young and in love," she said.

"What about you? All these years?" she asked.

"I eventually married. But it didn't work out," Tommy said.

"Children?" she asked.

"She couldn't, and then time goes by, and it's just too late," he said. "How many children did you have?" he asked.

"Three boys. All wonderful. But Brian, the middle one, is the most accessible and dependable when it comes to helping out with their father," she said.

Linda looked down at her cleavage. The skin was crepey. She was on the wrong side of time.

They wound up in bed back at Tommy's Condo. She laid her head on his chest, peppered with wiry gray hairs.

"I don't remember you having chest hair," Linda said.

"It came later," he said.

"I'm so glad we did. It was a long time coming," she said.

"I was a little nervous I wouldn't live up to expectations," Tommy chuckled, which got him coughing. It was a smoker's cough.

"Have you ever thought of quitting?" she asked.

"I do quit about every three months. I get through two weeks, and then I go back. I guess it's better than nothing," Tommy said.

"Why don't you try the patch?"

Tommy reached over and opened the top drawer of the nightstand. He pulled out a box of Nicoderm CQ.

"They don't really do it for me," Tommy said. "There's just no point anymore."

"Why? You're still young," she said. "Do it for me."

"For you? Anything. I'll give it another try," Tommy said.

They both knew he was lying.

Linda snuck into her brother's house at 2 a.m. She felt like a kid again, except her Dad wasn't waiting up in his favorite armchair smoking his pipe. Linda slipped off to bed but could not sleep. She was too excited about having Tommy in her life again.

Kristie woke Linda at 8:20 a.m. She held out the house phone. It was a quaint wall-mounted phone with an exceptionally long cord stretching in from the hallway. It just took moments for Linda to understand Brian's anxious pleas for her to return home. Gary had had a stroke. It wasn't enough that she had become Gary's nursemaid, but now he would come up with another ailment that would keep her away from Tommy. She packed her bag and took an early flight home.

Linda had planned to get back to Tommy as soon as the funeral was over. But Tommy had suddenly become aloof. She didn't understand why he would put up a distance now that she was free. Linda called Tommy to plan another trip home to see him. She'd lost 12lbs since the funeral and was able to fit into a size 10 again, not her High School size 6 but better than the last time she'd seen him. Linda was eager to be important again, wanted again. She'd had enough illness and sympathy.

It was Kristie that sat her down at the kitchen

table when she arrived. Kristie placed a cup of tea before Linda and told her about Tommy. Linda sat in stony silence. He was gone. Suicide. No one had thought to tell her in time for the funeral. No one, but Kristie had any idea there was a connection.

"His cousin, Shirley, said he'd been diagnosed with lung cancer 6 months ago," Kristie told Linda.

"Thank you," Linda said and left the house.

In her rental car, she made a few phone calls and finally reached the Realtor of Tommy's Condo. She was able to get a last-minute viewing of the Condo. She had missed the funeral, but she still needed to reach out to him, to say goodbye. Linda went through a McDonald's drive-thru, then pulled over and parked. She picked at the fries and drank a medium Diet Coke.

When she got to Tommy's, it was empty inside except for the Realtor. Linda asked for a little privacy. The Realtor stepped outside. Linda didn't know what she had expected, but she had expected something. On the heels of losing Gary, how could Tommy just vanish from her life like this? She moved from room to room, saying goodbye. Some of the rooms she'd never been in until now. In the living room, Linda saw something glint at the edge of the carpet and the baseboard.

She pulled free a Kleenex from the little packet in her purse and dabbed at the tears in her eyes, careful not to smudge her eye makeup. Linda squatted and picked up a tooth. She wiped a bit of flesh from it and placed it in the inner pocket of her Kate Spade. The

Realtor, a nervous man, entered the Condo and asked her if she was done. He had a young couple coming to look at the space at 2 p.m.

"Yes, I understand. Youth is impatient," Linda said.

"Ah, yes. Well, you know then."

# Liar

You don't know me. You may have read the news, but that doesn't tell you anything. Allow me to tell you a little about myself. I am Beckett Broadmoor. Beck, to my wife, Bex, to my colleagues and friends. And, of course, Becky to the bullies from Middle school through High School. I didn't want to carry my childhood and adolescence any further. I needed an escape. Working at McDonald's in our small town of Mount Vernon, Il., I knew I was meant for better stuff. When I turned 22, the Manager promoted me to Assistant Manager. The old assistant manager was going off to college. College was never an option for me. I came from a large, low-income family. When I was a kid, I use to steal sodas for my siblings from the carport up the street. We'd take them to the woods at the dead end of our street. We would drink the warm, fizzy soda, and crush the cans under our feet on a pad of concrete forgotten in the woods. The remnants of some construction that never saw the fruition of somebody's dream. The soda was not thirst-quenching, but the crumple of the can was satisfying. I never got caught.

    The promotion to a dead-end job was a sign that I needed to get out. I started applying to jobs in St. Louis. It didn't matter too much what the position was as long as I could lie my way into it. I Googled a resume and made some personal adjustments. I listed Kaskaskia College with a bachelor's degree in business management as my major. I was sure any prospects would be like me and not know a damn thing about Kaskaskia. It didn't take too long to get a bite.

    Mid-West Power, MWP Inc., invited me to town for an interview. I packed my clothes in a Hefty trash bag and threw it in the backseat of my 1972 gold Ford Pinto. I never went home.

    I found a crappy little apartment with a full complement of mice, but it was mine, and that's all that mattered. I slept on the floor and ate fast food when I ate. After a couple of paychecks, I bought a used mattress and found a folding chair in the dumpster behind the apartment complex. Furniture wasn't necessary as I never had company. At first, I was happy to have the role of Assistant Accountant. After a year, I felt the Accountant was superfluous. I began to plant the seeds of embezzlement. It was easy. Aaron trusted me to do most of the work, making an easy paycheck for him, and making him an easy target for me. I let the money build and cut sizable checks to Aaron. Then I went to the President/Owner of the company with my suspicions. Understandably, Eric was furious. He didn't dig any deeper into the facts than what I presented. I was promoted.

    I decided to furnish my new apartment. I needed some semblance of normality to entertain women. At first, it was difficult to part ways with my money. After the living room set, it was addictive that feeling of purchase power. I collected Crate and Barrel as well as Pottery Barn catalogs. I dreamt of the day I could afford to shop there. I pictured the house I would one day have and all of the items I would attain. These layouts and designs filled my head as I fell asleep at night. These items were beacons of success. They were talismans of the me I wanted to be.

    Rene was a force. We met at a networking event for Technology in St. Louis, hosted by the Regional Commerce and Growth Association (RCGA). I wasn't expecting anything more than an one nightstand as that was the status quo of these events. This month's meeting was at the Hilton. I was drinking sensibly when Rene came up to me and placed a single malt whiskey in my hand.

    "Thank you, but I have to drive," I said.

"No, you don't. I have a room booked here," she said.

Her confidence was a turn-on, although her being six years my senior was a bit of a detraction. Within the first 15 minutes of conversation, Rene had established our ages and middle names: Shari (29) and Reggie (23). These questions were a sort of filter for her. I asked her why she wanted to know these things.

"These are facts that tell you nothing," I said.

Rene looked coy and asked me if I knew what my porn name was.

"What is the name of your first pet?" she asked.

"It was a family dog named Queenie," I said.

"And what was the name of the street you grew up on?"

"Burncoate," I said.

"So, your porn name is Queenie Burncoate," she said.

We laughed.

"What's yours?"

"Bubbles Firelight," she said.

I wanted to feel in control, but Rene was definitely calling the shots. It was unexpectedly freeing. Two months later, I was popping the question. She had so much more than I had. A fast-track engagement filled with registries and showers was an avalanche of material goods. I was richer than I'd ever been, and it wouldn't take me too long to pay off that ring. The guest list was our first disagreement. She wanted a list of friends and family. I told her I had none. Rene was not buying that, and at the end of a 3-hour argument, we ordered takeout, and I gave her a list: my co-workers, my hairstylist, and the bartender at the Old Bailey bar. I finally caved and gave Rene the addresses for my parents and siblings. This sufficed. Rene didn't care about my past. She believed she loved me. I knew I was just a check-in box on her list of life. At 29, her biological clock was ticking. Not that I was interested in having kids, I wanted to be the kid. I made Rene promise not to ask questions about me from my family. I told her they made me uncomfortable, and I didn't know what types of things they might say. In the end, I enjoyed the mixed looks of envy and pride on their faces. However, it was tempered by my embarrassment of them.

When we opened our wedding gifts the next afternoon, finally clothed but still drinking champagne, it was apparent my family had done their shopping at the Dollar Store. One, I only knew my mother to shop at the Dollar Store and Goodwill. Since this was my wedding, she would spring for brand new and shop at the Dollar Store. She got us a cloudy pair of glass candelabras, it looked like she lifted them from a church, and two table settings of red melamine tableware. Red was Mom's idea of fancy. Rene and I already had a kitchen fully outfitted by Pottery Barn with fine china from Bernardaud. When I carted the gifts from our hotel room, at the Hilton, down to my new red Land Rover Discovery, I stopped at a housekeeping cart in the hallway and pitched my family's presents in with resentment. For my wedding, not even my wedding, they couldn't muster up the funds for a decent gift? I already paid for their hotel rooms at the Drury Inn. Couldn't they give something? As always, they managed to take and take. Mom went about the reception room collecting centerpieces from tables, even as people sat about talking. Dad set up camp at the open bar.

Renee traveled a lot for work. It didn't bother me. It gave me time to continue my pursuits, younger women. I was nursing a Laphroaig neat at the Old Bailey bar when Bonnie attacked. She lunged at me, spilling half her Cosmo down my shirt. I knew I was getting laid, which worked out pleasantly as she had always been one of the girls on my list from my first job at MWP, Inc. I left MWP, Inc., for a more lucrative position as a Financial Advisor at Edward Jones. I landed that job through a contact of Rene's, but still, the work came from me. I had to sweat it out whether they would run any kind of background check that revealed Kaskaskia was a sham. Plus, I was always studying for various security licenses. I owed so much to Rene, and I think that is why I was so compelled to cheat on her. I needed to level the playing field.
Reluctantly, I agreed that we could go back to my place. Bonnie's roommate was studying for the bar. It had been so long since I had something new. I wished I

could recharge as quickly as I did in my teens. I wanted to fuck her again. She started talking. I'd never regain my hard-on now.

"There's a nasty rumor about you at work, Bex. They say you might have gone the way of Aaron. Remember Aaron,?" Her body squirmed about like a worm out of the soil, lost on the sunbaked pavement. Unaware of the danger of just being there.

"Did you? Did you do it, Bex? You can tell me," she said. Her big eyes had too much eye makeup. Her lips were fat and red. I dropped my cigarette and wrapped my hands around her neck. I don't remember if there was much of a struggle. I think it went quickly. The lipstick had smeared from her mouth. I glanced down at the pillowcase. It was marked. I noticed the cigarette lolling on the sheets. I grabbed at it, but it had rolled down against her ass. Finally, I dug it up. There was a hole in the sheet. It was going to look like rape and murder, but it was just murder. I was going to have to clean this up. I looked over at the alarm clock, 4:14 a.m.

I couldn't replay the incident clearly in my mind. I remember feeling scared, trapped; then everything went a dull, cloudy red. It was something like when you rub your eyes hard and see that blotchy red light on the inside of your eyelids. The next thing I remember was that cigarette lolling on the sheets, but even then, the cigarette was larger than life until I could blink things clear. I was straddling her body. I knew she was dead before I looked at her face. However, when I did look at her face again, I was filled with fear and hatred. I hated her for dying in my bed for having the power to make me feel helpless.

    I couldn't just dig a hole in the backyard. I had to have a purpose that I could share with my wife. To be honest, Rene was so faithful I probably could have shared the secret of the murder with her, but the infidelity was not going to fly. It worked out well last night, as it worked out well now that Bonnie didn't have a car. I don't know how I would have gotten rid of a vehicle. Bed, Bath, and Beyond opened at 9 a.m. I got Egyptian cotton sheets, 1800 thread count, with deep pockets for our pillow top mattress. Then I crossed the plaza to Lowes. It felt good to spend all of this time away from the body. I bought the supplies to build an elevated garden. Back home, I labored, building the frame of the garden, and I found myself singing Amazing Grace. I have a considerable, deep voice. Before the advent of my Adam's apple, I sang in the St. Thomas Aquinas parish choir. My Mom was a good Catholic; she had hoped one of her ten kids would become a priest. No one did. The hymn was calming. It eased the knot in my stomach.

    I painted the pressure treated landscape timber a barn red. I got the bags of raised bed soil in position. The Bonnie tomato plants sat in the sun, waiting to be planted in our new garden. I waited for dark, and then I waited some more. Our house backed up to woods, but there was no point in taking stupid chances. I laid her down in the garden. The moonlight glinted off an oval-shaped gold locket. I took it from her neck. Inside the locket was a picture of a Benji-looking dog. I threw it in the hole with her and pocketed the locket. Renee would like it, and it was free.

The hard work was behind me. I enjoyed planting the garden. The yard looked much nicer, and we would have fresh tomatoes. Have you ever had a homegrown tomato? They are so sweet and juicy with just enough acidity to balance the taste. To truly enjoy a homegrown tomato, you have to eat it plucked straight from the vine. Give it a quick rinse with the hose. It is still warm. Apply just enough pressure with your teeth to break the skin for an explosion of flavor that fills your mouth with a lush flood, and the juice dribbles down your chin. As I considered the hunt for the perfect tomato, I wondered what effect Bonnie's body would have on the tomatoes. I would have wagered it would bring out too much acidity, but there was no one to wager against. Murder is lonely work. Of course, I was right. Those tomatoes were more acidic than sweet, but what a unique flavor.

Mom had a garden: tomatoes, cucumbers, dill, mint, basil, peppers, cabbage, green beans, and peas. I hated peas. Every chance I got, I plucked those peas and fed them to the dog. That mutt was a smart dog, let me tell you. She had a stupid name, Bagel. My younger siblings named her. They must have been hungry. We were always hungry. There just wasn't enough. I remember one time, Dad bought a chocolate and almond candy bar from some guy at work. He felt obligated cause this guy always bought several boxes of Girl Scout cookies from my sisters. So, here comes my Dad feeling like the generous hero with his lone candy bar. He handed the chocolate to my eldest sibling Kurt. A fight broke out in that tiny living room. Dad became invisible to us. We tore that room apart, trying to get to that chocolate. Kurt was a good head taller than all of us, but we took him down. In the end, most of us got a bit of chocolate. A few of us got bit for our trouble. The youngest got nothing. Dad said he'd never bring a candy bar like that home again. He still sold the Girl Scout cookies at work, and he continued to buy one candy bar from his co-worker. It was just now he ate it in his car on his way home from work. It was for the best; I didn't like nuts in my chocolate anyway.

    It was good to see Rene. I had gone to Hobby Lobby and bought a generic little jewelry box and some red ribbon to wrap her gift. I had it sitting on the passenger seat of the Land Rover. I put her luggage in the back as she climbed in the front. She had been mid-sentence telling me nothing I needed to hear, going on about an annoying co-worker at the conference. Rene stopped mid-sentence at the sight of the box.

    "Can I open it?"
    "It's for you," I said.
    "Oh, Beck. It's beautiful."

"You will have to get a picture to put in it."

"I'm going to call your mom and get a picture of you as a boy," she said.

I was regretting the locket already.

When we got home, I was starting with a migraine. I went straight to bed and woke in the early evening. Rene was too chatty, excited about the locket, and the elevated garden. Apparently, I had done well while she was out of town.

"And I had been concerned for you being home alone," she said.

Entangled in the sheets, Rene and I were pillow talking.

"You know how I told you I was racing cars in my early twenties?"

"Yes, you did autocross driving."

"Well, did I tell you about the time I got into a fistfight with a member of one of the other cars' pit crew?"

"No, why?"

I knew I hadn't told her the story, because I hadn't made it up yet.

"I had a girl in my pit crew. She was great at changing tires. Well, this guy from another pit crew makes a real vulgar comment about her. He did it all the time, but this time it just put me off. I grabbed a mallet, marched over and slung that mallet across his knees. I busted one of his knee caps," I said.

"Oh, my God! What happened?"

"He went to the hospital. Everyone was glad someone finally shut him up. I did feel a little bad later. I didn't want to hurt someone, but I had to stand up for my crew."

"All of this happened down in Mount Vernon?"

"Yea, that's one of the reasons I don't like to go home. I don't like to think of myself like that, but I was good at race car driving."

I wasn't worried about my story. There was no way she knew more about race car driving than I did. I watched it on TV with my Dad. I'd watch it intently. My brothers and sisters were rowdy, rolling around the floor and wrestling like a pack of dogs.

Although I was a financial advisor, I handled my own money poorly. I didn't like to save. I wanted to spend, spend, spend. Rene was too accommodating and trusting.

One Saturday afternoon, I went out and bought a Harley Davidson. I had to go home and pick Rene up and drive back out to the dealership. I told her that I had just stopped in to look and was feeling nostalgic for the Hog I had in the early 90s. The one I had wrecked and wound up with all those medical bills. I was the innocent bystander in a high-speed car chase. The story was a lie to get the bike. The hospital bills were real enough from a drinking and driving accident I had in the Pinto. I didn't tell her that. But it was how I explained my piece of shit replacement car when we met, a Mazda 626 light blue, with one brown door.

Now, I had the Land Rover and a Harley. Rene was good for me.

Rene was picking tomatoes for a salad. I was grilling the steaks. Max, our Australian Shepherd, was sitting in the sun. The idea of getting a dog was my impulsive decision. Rene wanted a golden doodle. I told her the "story" of the Australian Shepherd I'd had as a kid, and for some unknown reason, he'd run off one day. His name was Max.

Sometimes it amused me how she bought my lies. It made me feel smarter, better than her. Rene adopted every story I told her and made it a part of the tapestry of us.

"Max, stop it," she said.

The dog was nosing around the elevated garden again. I'd been working with Max to stay away from the tomato garden. He was better at listening to me than Rene. I needed him to back off. I didn't want to have to put him down. He was a good dog. I felt protected with him around.

There was an increase in Rene's travel; it came with a promotion. She was earning three times what I brought home. I talked to a co-worker, and we agreed to go in on some property together. We were slum lords, but we felt like kings. I told Rene about our philanthropic efforts, which provided an excellent framework to hide the money. The money coming in was plentiful. I had to interpolate the funds in the columns on the ledger. I needed another business venture. I was looking for a loser. The tax shelter came in the form of an Angel Investment. I could have put the money in a retirement account, but I never planned that far ahead, and I wanted the money to be more fungible. As an Angel Investor, I could always pull out. I became an Angel Investor for a delivery service. Even this was a successful venture, and I was facing taxes that I had not put aside.

A creature of habit, I continued to drink my problems away at the Old Bailey bar. Stan, the bartender, was still there.

"Stan, don't you ever get a day off?"

Mixing someone a Rusty Nail, "Rarely, but I need the money, you know," Stan said.

I'd gotten to know Stan over the years. Most of his money was going up his nose. I could never understand this flagrant waste of money.

No one ever mentioned Bonnie. It was too easy and too tempting. I was fishing in the Old Bailey pond again. This time Rene was in Vegas with her college girlfriends. It was somebody's birthday. They were going for Margaritas and Botox injections as much as the gambling and shows.

Ashley Davis was playing pool badly. Her ass looked good enough to eat when she bent over the corner pocket to take a shot. I was torn between watching the show and inserting myself in the picture.

A bulked-up, muscular guy was jockeying for position as well. He'd taken the cue from her to show off his skills. He sunk the ball and himself. I introduced myself. I knew the score. I bought her a drink and praised her. I didn't play my best. I stroked her ego, and I was unassuming. I had a trendy haircut and nice but not flashy clothes. I was of a slender, muscular build, attractive, and not intimidating.

Ashley was zaftig, just enough to still be pretty and squeezable. And she was self-aware enough to let her guard down to be selected. Ashley was looking to get laid by a nice man. I acquiesced.

The dog was crated. Ashley was agreeable. I'd forgotten how fun girls with low self-esteem were. They'd let you do anything. I wanted to role-play. I tried to choke her, just a little. Just to get the feel of it, but she panicked. She scratched me on the chest. Her nails made my left nipple bleed. I got angry and squeezed harder. Ashley's face was turning blue; it was complimentary to her bugging blue eyes. I don't think I could have stopped if I wanted to, but I simply didn't want to. I kept choking her after she died. I tried to get more out of it. I wanted that high.

I did cum inside her while I was choking her, but I was still pent-up. I dismounted and paced the room, thumping my chests with my fists. My nostrils flared with deep breathing. When I returned to the bed to get some sleep, I slid her body over to Rene's side; I discovered that Ashley had urinated. I stripped the sheets and laundered them. I took a shower. Ashley lay on the bedroom floor, her glassy eyes wide open. She looked like one of my sister's dolls. Those dolls were always naked, lying on the floor, staring wide-eyed at the ceiling. I always thought dolls were creepy. A truck never looked like that; it never asked to be choked. I strut the room, telling Ashley what for as I smoked a cigarette. I just had to be sure to get the smell of the smoke out before Rene came home. I put my cigarette out in Ashley's navel, that was funny. I wasn't allowed to smoke in the house. I was relegated to the deck. I set my alarm. I had to build another elevated garden in the morning.

I liked to cook. I got to be creative, and I could look out the kitchen window to see the elevated gardens. I planted big Lilac shrubs. Three of them fit quite nicely. I planted some lavender all around the outside border. Purple was Rene's favorite color.

"Dinner's ready," I said.

She entered from the office.

"Making any progress?" I asked.

"It is just a cluster fuck. I have to go through all of last year's spreadsheets to make sense of productivity. But something sure does smell good," she said.

"Oxtail stew, your favorite," I said.

"You are a saint. I think it is your cooking I miss most when I'm on the road," she said.

"Wine with dinner?"

"Always. I'll get it," she said.

Max sat curled at my feet while we supped. He

got everything I dropped. He was better than the Roomba.

"David called. He wants to go fishing," I said.

"You should go. When?"

"This weekend," I said.

"Go, you never go out with your friends," she said.

She failed to realize I didn't have any friends. They were all her friends.

"Yeah, maybe I will."

Rene cleared the table and did the dishes. I went out on the deck for a smoke. I didn't want to go fishing. Rene thought I loved fishing because I told her I use to love it as a boy. It was a lie, of course. I watched Max sniff around the lavender and lilac. I couldn't go even if I wanted to. I had to keep an eye of this dog. If I left him alone with Rene, she'd leave him alone in the yard long enough to dig one of the girls up. I suddenly realized I was saddled to this yard, house. We could never sell. What if the new owners dug up the gardens? I'd made myself a prison. How was I going to get out?

I told another lie to Rene and David to get out of the fishing trip. I stayed home and went through all the paperwork in the office, all of our financials. Rene thought I was fastidious. I was paranoid—the bodies in the backyard, the shuffling of funds. I needed Rene to go on another business trip. As I fanned out some of the paperwork, I came across our life insurance policies. Rene was insured for a lot of money. I put the file back.

I didn't want to think about that.

It was a sunny day. I was tending to the gardens. I felt tethered to the gardens. Rene came out on the deck. "Beck, did you get a passport?"

It had finally come in the mail.

"It was supposed to be a surprise. I've been planning a trip for us," I said.

"Where?" She skipped across the yard to me.

"Cabo," I said. It was the first thing I could think of.

"When?"

"Um, I'm not sure. I didn't know when you could get away," I said. It had become so easy to lie to Rene

It was three weeks later. Rene found me moping in the living room.

"What's wrong," she said with a bottle of Pledge and a dust rag in her hands.

"Peter died."

"Oh, no. I never even got to meet him," she said.

"He was my best friend in high school," I said. She knew that, but what she did not realize was Peter was in a band in high school, a heavy metal band. I was not. In fact, the real Peter didn't even know I existed.

"What did he die of?"

"Cancer."

"When is the funeral?"

"We missed it. His wife wanted it over quickly," I said.

"That's weird," Rene said.

She had no idea how weird. Peter was alive and well and divorced. I followed him on Facebook. Rene held my hand. I started singing a hymn, softly crying. I was moored by my own lies. The lines between reality and fantasy blurred.

It was becoming difficult to track my lies. I was nervous. I didn't like the unsettled feeling I'd lived with as a child catching up to me in all of my success. I had to gain control. It would be months before I had the balls to do what was necessary. But winter was coming, and I could not afford to wait till the ground froze. I had paid the taxes owed in the spring. I had moved some things around. I was selling the slums for cash.

It was a Friday night, as that gave me the most time. I initiated sex. It was easy to get into position. She liked missionary, which had always worked for us. I wanted to be in control. I waited for her to cum, and then I wrapped my hands around her neck. I knew how much pressure it would take, but I was having a hard time exerting the full force. I didn't want to kill her. I started to cry as she gasped. My vision was murky, and a hand slipped free. Rene reached back and to the left of the headboard. She grabbed my second-grade soccer trophy. I had told her that we won that year that I was attached to it. Really, I had picked the trophy up at an antique store. She hit me in the head just over the left eyebrow.

"That's my trophy," I said. Blood spurted. It

reinforced my commitment to kill her. I knocked the trophy from her hand and placed my hands around her throat again. I started crying.

"Not you. The others were fun. But you are my wife. I'm sorry. I'm so sorry."

Rene began to shudder and then fell limp. There was some of my blood on her face. I cleaned up. I had run out of room in the backyard. So, I put her in the burn pit behind the shed. I had to use an accelerant to get it hot enough. I stood by, naked, smoking a pack of cigarettes watching the fire. I sang Amazing Grace. The fire had burned higher and brighter than I anticipated. I hoped no one would see the flames and call the cops. I was betting on the remote nature of our home to give me cover. I dug up both elevated gardens and added Bonnie and Ashley to the burn pit. When the fire had burned out, I shoveled up the ashes and put them back in the elevated gardens. I replanted the Bonnie tomatoes and the Lilac and Lavender. Both beds looked ruffled, but I felt much more comfortable. I felt like I could leave.

I had to walk, no run from the life insurance money. It was a lot of money, but too risky. I was going to be the number one suspect. I spent Saturday at the spa we frequented. I got a new haircut from my stylist and a massage from Kyle. He worked wonders on my back and shoulders. Sunday, I checked that my funds had been moved to a new account. I knew it was a done deal. But I couldn't help but double-check. I packed a small suitcase with clothes and my passport. I headed somewhere that doesn't extradite. I set up a shop as a photographer at a 3-star hotel right on the beach. I seduced the widows looking for romance after nursing spouses with lingering illnesses and substantial life insurance policies. I just had a way with older women. I never strangled a woman again. It wasn't worth it. I could just fuck it out of them.

# Swimming Middle River

## ACKNOWLEDGEMENTS:

- Somebody Else In Kentucky appeared in Blacktop Passages
- The Family Blend appeared in Crack the Spine
- A Point of Departure was published in Connotation Press
- Burnt Prairie was published in Halfway Down the Stairs
- Man in Black appeared in The Writing Disorder
- Swimming Middle River was published in Momaya

## ABOUT THE AUTHOR

Leah Holbrook Sackett is a short story writer. Swimming Middle River is her first book. In it, the reader traverses the protagonists' journey toward autonomy. Her characters face ever-mounting boundaries from society, family, and self, which leads them to a crossroads of decision. Leah is also an adjunct lecturer in the English department at the University of Missouri - St. Louis. This is where she earned her B.A. in English and M.F.A. in creative writing.

https://leaholbrooksackett.com/

**Also by REaDLips Press:**

How to Throw a Psychic a Surprise Party

by Noreen Lace

The Lone Escapist by Dan Rhys

I, Polyphemus by Ron Terranova

The Last Night in Granada by Chris Pellezzari

Made in the USA
Monee, IL
09 August 2020